THE
JOURNEY OF
TWELVE
AND
SNAKEWOLFE

THE
JOURNEY OF
TWELVE
AND
SNAKEWOLFE

JOSEPH RICHARD SEES

THE JOURNEY OF TWELVE AND SNAKEWOLFE

iUniverse books may be ordered through booksellers or by contacting:

iUniverse
1663 Liberty Drive
Bloomington, IN 47403
www.iuniverse.com
1-800-Authors (1-800-288-4677)

Because of the dynamic nature of the Internet, any web addresses or links contained in this book may have changed since publication and may no longer be valid. The views expressed in this work are solely those of the author and do not necessarily reflect the views of the publisher, and the publisher hereby disclaims any responsibility for them.

Any people depicted in stock imagery provided by Getty Images are models, and such images are being used for illustrative purposes only.
Certain stock imagery © Getty Images.

ISBN: 978-1-5320-6151-6 (sc)
ISBN: 978-1-5320-6152-3 (e)

Print information available on the last page.

iUniverse rev. date: 10/29/2018

Chapter 1

HOME FOR LUNCH

There was a boy who loved sports his name was Twelve. Twelve lived on N9999 E St, in a little house with a broken window that Twelve's dad Jack was fixing. His mother Jacky was cooking lunch for the three of them.

"Jack!" called Jacky.

"Yes, Jacky what is it?" Jack answered.

"Dinner is done and Twelve will be home soon" Jacky called again.

"K" Jack answered.

Five minutes later, Twelve pulled into the driveway in his mom's car, which was an old volts wagon from the year 2000 in the year 2040. When Twelve pulled into the driveway him and his mom exchanged greetings.

"Hi mom how are you today on this fine day?" Twelve said with a very happy grin on his face.

"I'm fine but your father needs your help" Jacky said while rolling her eyes and smiling.

"K, but what has he done now" Twelve answered also rolling his eyes, but smiling as well.

"He broke the window earlier this afternoon and now he is trying to fix it." Jacky answered back.

After Twelve talked with his mother, he went to talk to his dad.

"You are always trying to fix something that you have broken when I come home, why do you always break something dad, are you always angry or something?" Twelve asked with disbelief in his voice."

"Just have a knack for it I guess." Jack answered shrugging his shoulders.

"Alright what do you need me to do?" Twelve asked his dad walking up to him with a grin.

"I need you to hold the window in so I can get it into place." Jack answered.

"Like this dad?" Twelve asked looking at his father innocently

He took the window and shoved it into place for his dad.

"Hey, do you ever stop being so amazing?" Jack asked while laughing.

"Nope, I try to impress you and mom." Twelve said while laughing alongside his father.

"Well you do a good job at that!" His parents said at the same time.

"Thanks mom, thanks dad I feel super appreciated by both of you. What's for lunch, wait let me smell my way to the kitchen. I smell, chicken with a dash of butter and lemon sauce my favorite." Twelve said with a smile on his face.

"I swear you have a canine's sense of smell and hearing Twelve's mom said. Speaking of hearing, the washer and dryer are making that squeaking sound again." Jacky said looking at Jack.

"I will get it after lunch Jacky. I promise." Twelve's dad said while trying not crack a smile, because he knew Jacky was being serious.

They ate lunch in silence and Twelve went back to school afterwards. On his way to school, he saw a car accident and he stopped to check it out. A scream came from the nearest car. Twelve went to check on the woman that screamed and she had a broken leg. He pulled her out and tied two pieces of wood on her leg as a splint to hold the leg together. The worst thing possible happened. Another car came speeding around the corner and was about to hit the woman, Twelve ran forward and pushed her out of the way with one second to spare. He spun around, put his right foot down as if he was getting ready to tackle someone, and smashed both his hands onto the hood of the man's car and he didn't flinch.

The man got out of his car ready to fight. In fact he threw the first punch. Twelve was about to put his hand up when he heard sirens and heard another cry for help. He ducked and ran to the red car; this time there was a woman with ten kids between 3 and 10 years old.

"Are you injured!?" Twelve asked the woman while pulling her out of the car.

"No, I'm not injured but my ten-year-old son is." The woman said while panicking

Twelve ducked into the red car that was up side down. After getting the woman out he went back for the children. When he got back, the five smallest kids grabbed onto him like there was no tomorrow. He took them out and they ran to their mother. He went into the car and the four other kids did the same thing. He brought them out and they ran to their mother as well. Before he got back to the car for the last time, it started on fire. He jumped into the car and his clothes caught on fire. The fire was burning through his clothes which in tern started burning his skin it was very bad. If Twelve had not been as tough as he was he probably would have been yelling and screaming from the pain. Nevertheless, he ignored that and grabbed the ten year old. There was a loud click and he broke open the back window with a couple of kicks and threw the kid out. A miller second later it blew up. In the explosion, Twelve's whole body was in flames the people that he saved tried to put the fire out but did not succeed in doing so before the ambulance got there.

Chapter 2

THE AMBULENCE AND HOSPITAL

When the ambulance got there, Twelve had saved everyone but himself. When the car blew up he was lying face down, severely burnt around his shoulders and back. On the way to the hospital Twelve woke up and asked for a mirror. He was afraid he wouldn't be able to play sports because of what he might look like after he healed from his accident. His mom started to give him the mirror but the nurse snatched it out of her hand. The nurse and his mom started arguing.

"If my son wants to see his face then he gets what he wants!" Jacky was yelling.

The nurse was saying that she was not going to allow him to see himself until he was in the hospital.

The driver for the ambulance stopped ten feet from the Hospital because he could sense that Twelve was going to shout.

Give me the mirror now!" Twelve shouted and practically swore, which showed how angry he was.

The nurse gave him the mirror shaking horribly because she had never been yelled at like that before. She was scared out of her mind.

"I will be able to play sports no problem right? I mean, my back couldn't possibly be that bad right? What does my back look like anyway?" Twelve asked starting to get concerned from looking at his parents faces.

"son haven't you noticed that you're lying on your stomach?" Jack asked, noticing that Twelve didn't notice that he was on his stomach.

"Is it truly that bad dad?" Twelve asked trying to fight back the tears because his adrenaline rush had worn off.

"Yes son, yes it is that bad." Jack said with an unhappy look on his face while choking on the words coming out of his mouth.

"How long until I can walk again a year or maybe two right, I mean I won't be in a wheelchair for the rest of my life will I?" Twelve asked with tears running down his face.

"As far as we can tell, it is very possible that you might be in a wheelchair for the rest of your life." His dad answered unable to look his dad in the face.

"What?! Are you serious?!" Twelve shouted in surprise and anger at the same time.

"See I told you that Twelve would act like this if we told him the truth about his back; I told you he would take it like this. He may be stronger than normal people, but he wasn't strong enough for

3

the truth. Besides, the chances that he will be able to walk again are a billion to one." The nurse said without missing a beat.

Twelve's mother walked up to the nurse looked her in the eye for exactly one minute and she punched the nurse two times so hard that she broke her nose and her ribs on the right side of the nurse's body. The nurse spat blood all over the ambulance floor. Jacky went to punch the nurse some more but Jake stopped her before she got close enough. He held her for the rest of the ambulance ride.

When they arrived at the hospital, they put him in a safety bed so he would lay flat on his stomach and not hurt anyone else because he had a seizure and accidentally hurt another nurse. His friends came and visited him but he was sad. He read all of his books, did his homework and the only thing he could do was stay in the bed or in the wheelchair. It was September 3 2041 when it happened. This person came in the hospital to visit him and his name was Nargrader the great. He was like 7 feet tall between 100-220 pounds, and he had a very, very deep voice.

"Twelve it's time to go back home. We need you to save us from the monsters from the realm of Nightmares that Nightmare created." Nargrader asked while walking around to the right side of Twelve's bed.

"I told you that I didn't understand what you meant the first time you visited me and asked me for help. There's no such thing as Nightmare or monsters or even for that matter other worlds. Why are you coming to me with your problems? I'm very confused." Twelve asked in a very confused way.

"I'll explain everything step by step." Nargrader said with a very concerning smile on his face.

"About 5,000 years ago, there was a boy whose name was Twelveontia, he came to my world, he brought us tools, magic, games, and he gave us names and weapons to protect ourselves. Before he came to our world all of our names were Nobody, each person was called Nobody, and one individual who was named Noxmondamon started studying the dark magic and made spells that he used to kill people. They were very terrible and powerful spells, but he wanted more power. He went to the cave that Twelveontia lived in and they started to fight. At the end of the battle, Twelve made a prophecy that one day he would return and save everyone and that the blade of heaven would return once again to the chosen one. The blade will pick the one that will not use it for darkness. Noxmondamon took all the secrets from Twelve's dying hand and began creating a purple ball that consumed him and he was gone. My people and I thought he was gone forever, but he has come back with these monsters and we do not know what to do or even how to fight them." Nargrader said, still wearing that concerning smile, like he was about to win a prize or something.

"So let me get this straight, you want my help because I am the one who was chosen to save your world, by me, 5,000 years ago?" Twelve asked with a look on his face as if his eyes were going to pop out of their sockets. (There's no way that Nargrader is telling me everything, and look at his smile, he's totally a bad guy. I think he's making everything up as he goes along. No matter what he says, weather it's true or not, doesn't matter because if there are people who really are in trouble, then I must do what I can to save them, no matter what it takes.)

"Yes, however there is a catch. You see, the the catch is that you might have to save your world as well." Nargrader said with that same smile. (Adding the part about having to save his own world as well, just might have set the hook line and sinker, for me to actually get this idiot to believe that he is the savior.)

Chapter 3

THE NEW WORLD

"The new world was just like my own world but there was one different thing, it was full of monsters just like Nargrader said. All right I believe you now, but what am I supposed do?" Twelve asked while spinning around in his wheelchair.

However, when he spun around Nargrader was gone. There was a note in his pocket.

Dear Twelve

I stuck this note in your pocket for two reasons and the first one is the list of creatures and their names and where you could get a shield, a weapon and armor.

Twelve took out the first part of the note and there were at least 10 pages of names with at least 500 names per list. He skimmed through the list and realized that it was not just names but also a definition of their power and what kind of magic as well. The second one was a map of the area he was in and a bag of 10 pounds of dust. He read the rest of the note.

The pounds of dust are how we pay for stuff around here. The dust came to be when Nightmare came.

Nargrader

PS: If you stay in one spot for to long, you may be attacked by a monster.

When he turned around, he was attacked. He did not have a sword and he was in a wheel chair. The first thing he did was punch the Roller eye. It looked like an eye that could not stop itself from rolling around in a circle. When he punched it, he killed it, after he killed it he noticed some dust on the ground. He picked it up and then went to the nearest town shown on the map. When he got to the town, he stopped in front of the gate. It was at least 30 feet high and 30 feet thick. There was a man asleep in the tower on the top.

"Hey you up there, wake up, and please open the door!" Twelve shouted loudly.

A hand and a half sword fell out of the tower he went to pick it up and noticed there was blood on the sword. As soon as he picked it up, he realized what he had to do. Before he dug the sword into the ground he strapped himself to the wheelchair and then he grabbed the handle and used it to fling himself at the wall. It worked and he was having fun. When he hit the wall, he dug his fingers into it and started climbing. When he got to the top, he saw what had happened to the town.

Without thinking, he took the sword and stuck it into the wall and slid down, riding the wall with the wheels on his wheelchair causing sparks that followed him all the way to the ground. His wheelchair started screeching in protest at the speed that he was going. As soon as he hit the ground he started looking for survivors. He started to listen and heard a cling in the background. He turned right at the first corner. Twelve wheeled in-between the two men and caught the blades in mid blow.

"What is the meaning of this fight?" Twelve shouted because he hates it when people fight. (What in the hell is happening to me? I can't believe I just caught those swords with my bare hands, this is unbelievable and super cool.)

"My name is X-Heart Xnomez, this person is One Eye Red Eye, and he killed my family and the people in this town, my town." The man on the right said trying to stay calm enough to answer the question.

Twelve let go of the swords and let them continue fighting. When the battle was over X-Heart Xnomez had won.

"Mr. X-Heart Xnomez I would like to shake your hand if that's okay with you." Twelve asked extending his hand out to be friendly.

X-Heart Xnomez took Twelve's hand and when they shook hands, Twelve saw into his past and trusted the man even though his name sounded evil. He helped the smith rebuild the town of armory and swordsmanship. X-Heart Xnomez thanked him and gave him a sword, which was a long sword and a shield made of a mythical metal called Stalagshneer and it, is the strongest metal in the world.

"Thank you very much but why not have me pay for these items? Aren't they expensive?" Twelve asked, trying to give them back so he could pay for them like a normal customer

"You helped me so I've decided that I would help you in return, but mind you, I will make you pay for it next time you decide to come to me for a sword and shield." X-Heart answered with a smile of friendship on his face.

"X- Heart, do you know a man named Nargrader?" Twelve asked, seeing if Xnomez would be able to help him.

"No, I do not, but I Know a man named Yackmacknarbog and he lives in the cave over there behind the town and up that hill. However, there was also a herd of Nagragkillers on their way to the cave. The heard had at least 400 Nagragkillers in it and that is about nine thousand pounds of dust." Xnomez answered, hoping that in some way he was able to help Twelve again.

Twelve started walking toward the cave with a greedy grin on his face but X-Heart Xnomez pulled him back by the sleeve of his shirt.

"What's the matter?" Twelve asked with a look of confusion on his face.

"There weakness is fire, do you know any magic?" Xnomez asked, while looking at him like he's crazy for going to the cave to kill 400 Nagragkillers without magic.

"No, I don't know how to use magic, but could you teach me?" Twelve asked, hoping that he could learn magic quickly.

"No, I cannot, you have to go to the store on the corner and knock on the door, for magic." Xnomez answered in an apologetic way.

When he went to the store, the owner of the store had closed and locked the door during the sword fight. He knocked three times. When the door opened, the owner looked like he had been sleeping.

"w-what is it?" The owner asked while trying to stop himself from yawning.

"I am Twelve and I was wondering if you could teach me how to use magic?" Twelve asked with some excitement in his voice.

O-o-o-of course, my name is Battle-gargantuan, now what kind of magic would you like to learn?" Battle-gargantuan, asked surprised that he finally met somebody who was excited about magic.

The first thing Twelve and Gargantuan did was walk into the magic store. Twelve walked around looking at the prices for Fire, Blizzard, Thunder, and Cure, then he went and measured 12 pounds of dust. After that battle he had with the Roller Eye he made 110 pounds of dust which gave him 120 pounds of dust total. Twelve paid the 12 pounds of dust and they got to work. It took him four hours per spell. The first spell he learned was cure. The true name of cure is Heelareia. He used it to heel his wounds from when he fought the Roller eye. The second spell was fire. The true name for fire is Burnasha. The third spell was blizzard. The true name for blizzard is Frezzear.

"What if I just said Frez, instead of the whole spell?" Twelve asked with a very curious look on his face.

"It will hit the spell caster and hurt them really badly." Gargantuan replied with a scowl.

They started on the fourth spell thunder. The true name for thunder is Thundragar.

"Twelve you are ready to face the Nagragkillers but remember do not use any other spell on Nagragkillers accept Burnasha and wait for it to lay on its back, then strike." Gargantuan reminded him before he left.

Chapter 4
THE CAVE

When Twelve got to the cave, the man that he had heard of was under attack by the heard of Nagragkillers. Twelve made a sound of frustration and the Nagragkillers all turned around and fell on their backs because he surprised them. Twelve cast the spell Burnasha on all of them and they flipped back on all fours. Twelve moved to the nearest Nagragkiller and with the sword he had, he cast Burnasha on his sword. It worked and he cast all of his spells onto his sword accept Heelareia. When he mixed the spells together, they formed a spell called Element-all When Yackmacknarbog saw the sword, a Nagragkiller hit him in the chest and he fell down. Twelve wheeled to his side and the Nagragkillers flipped onto their backs. Twelve concentrated all his speed into one attack. Considering that he is in a wheel chair, it wasn't easy. Then again, he technically is not a normal human. When he did his attack, he yelled out, Speedy Slice Of Hell! Because of his sword, his attack was 10 times as powerful as Burnasha when he cast it on all of them. One by one, the Nagragkillers all died and Twelve picked up the dust. After Twelve killed all the Nagragkillers, he went to Yackmacknarbog.

"If you had kept casting Burnasha, it would have taken four more hits to kill them all." Yackmacknarbog said wiping his forehead off because he had been nervous

Twelve just replied that it would have been more fun.

"What? Are you mad? Why do you love to fight?" Yackmacknarbog asked with a bit of force in his voice when he asked the question.

"I love to fight because I fight to save the people of the world not to kill and be evil." Twelve answered with a smile on his face, happy with his answer.

Twelve turned around and started to make sure he had collected all of the dust after he said that. At that specific moment Yackmacknarbog's skin melted right off. Yackmacknarbog was a Mocking-Parnassus, a creature that if killed you gain 200 pounds of dust but they only pop out of their hiding place when they want to battle someone. These creatures are very dangerous, so if you fight one you should have at least four people in your group. I know what you are thinking and Twelve has not been hurt yet. Twelve faced the Mocking-Parnassus and realized that it was standing on two legs, had four heads, three arms, and horrible breath. Just for the simple fact that Twelve was in a wheel chair, he let the Mocking-Parnassus attack first. It walked up to him and swallowed him whole. He did nothing at all. The inside of a Mocking-Parnassus' stomach is full of an acid that if drank would melt your body from the inside out unless you were poisoned by a giant baby scorpion. Twelve was just sitting in his wheelchair and he said release me you beast and I will not kill you. For some reason it did, what Twelve asked and puked him up.

After he was out, he had his eyes closed. The Mocking-Parnassus licked him clean. She looked at Twelve and Twelve looked back. They stared at each other for an hour.

"Would you become my friend?" Twelve asked the Mocking-Parnassus, smiling at her.

"She answered at first with a roar to clear her throat, and it slowly became wards, yes human named Twelve I will be your friend but I'm a baby." Mocking-Parnassus answered smiling back at Twelve.

"May I call you Sarus?" Twelve asked. (If Mocking-Parnassus is a baby, how big is an adult one.)

"Yes, yes Twelve you may call me Sarus. It is a wonderful name I love it." Mocking-Parnassus answered, running outside and jumping for joy almost causing an earth quake.

Sarus and Twelve went to the village. When they got there, the people in the town were surprised. A little boy started running towards Twelve and Sarus. Twelve instantly ran forward and picked the boy up off the ground.

"The boy's mother went up to Twelve and asked, will you spare my son my lord? He is only six and he has not been in his first battle." The woman pleaded getting on her hands and knees

"Twelve, your not in your wheelchair anymore, that must mean that you're all healed up." Sarus said gasping for breath from the excitement of seeing him get out of his chair.

"I am not Nightmare ma'am. My name is Twelve and I do not plan to hurt your son." Twelve said while walking up to the poor woman and helping her up off the ground. (She's right, I'm not in my wheelchair anymore, sweet.)

You aren't going to hurt my son? The Woman asked finally looking at Twelve, realizing that he wasn't Nightmare.

"Nope, I will not hurt your son. The reason I stopped him is because he was going to hurt my friend, oh what did you say his name was? Twelve asked.

"My son's name Sir I did not say what his name was. Would you like to know what his name is?" The woman asked beginning to wonder who exactly Twelve was, and why he was in her town.

"Yes I would." Twelve answered.

"His name is SnakeWolfe." the woman answered.

"Would his father have been SnakeWolfe the first?" Twelve asked hoping that the woman wouldn't say yes.

"Yes, it is and he is not hear, I do not know where he is." The woman said answered with surprise from the look on Twelve's face when she told him the answer.

"I do, I know where SnakeWolfe is. He's dead, he died in my world. Before you say anything please let me explain?" Twelve asked the town hoping that they would let him explain what happened.

"Please explain what happened to him!" The entire town shouted at the same time.

"SnakeWolfe and I got in a fight over who would drive me home after I got out of the hospital. He tried to punch me in the head and my instant reaction was to defend myself. I punched him in the chest with all my strength. The doctor tried to save him but I hit his chest and dented it in. He died in my arms while I was in my wheelchair. The last thing he said to me was, to let his son on my team. I Twelve the nicest person in my world was called a murderer and I said yes to SnakeWolfe's request. Twelve explained."

You killed my father... After SnakeWolfe Junior said that, he started yelling. AAAAAAAAAA AAAAAAAAAAAAAAAAAAAAAAAAAAAAAAAAAAAAAAAAAAAAAAAAAAAAAAAAAAAAAAAA

AAAAAAAAAAAAAAAAAAAAAAAAAAAAAAAH! When he finally stopped yelling, two swords popped into his hands. One flaming with red Burnasha and the other flaming with blue Burnasha. The names of the swords were, Raging-Flame-Agra and Blue-Furnasha. These swords heal the person who wields them in battle. Every fight he is in, every battle he is in, he can win. The swords heal his wounds, no matter how great it is. With these swords, SnakeWolfe attacked Twelve.

Twelve let him attack. When SnakeWolfe struck Twelve, he flew through the wall behind him.

"Do not attack him Sarus it is not his fault but mine. Now I need you to help me up please." Twelve said, while being unable to move from such a powerful attack.

Sarus went and picked him up by the collar.

"I will join your team but you need to teach me how to do all the moves that my father knew." SnakeWolfe said with a grin of happiness on his face, he was happy because he would follow his father's footsteps.

"You already know all that stuff because you just did one of his attacks. You see he based his attacks on his emotions. Which were mostly when he was angry or when he thought of something to anger him. He had such good control of his emotions that most of the time when you saw him, he looked blank. He had an extremely amazing talent, a talent that you might have as well. The ability to feel other people's emotions. You see, your father fed off of that. When the people around him were happy he would be happy, and vice versa with anger. Being able to do this made using his powers a lot easier for him." Twelve said while finally being able to move again.

"So his attacks were more powerful when he was angry." SnakeWolfe said with a smile, while hugging his mother.

"Exactly answered a familiar voice that came from behind Twelve. Twelve I am surprised you are still alive. In this world, I thought you would have been as dumb and foolish as you were in your own world. I still can't believe that you would risk your life for a bunch of people that you don't even know." Nargrader said in that deep voice that he had that annoyed everybody. Twelve answered with his sword. He swung his sword at Nargrader but just landed it on his neck and he did not make him bleed but gave him a cut that he would not forget."

"I thought you would cut my head off." Nargrader said with an angry look on his face."

"I Twelve will not execute you, but I must ask. Does it burn at all, that cut I gave you?" Twelve asked with a half-smile half grin on his face.

"Yes, yes it does Twelve. I'm usually pretty good with using spells, however I don't know any spell that can get rid of this cut, do you?" Nargrader asked knowing very well that he would know, but wouldn't help him.

"Yes, I do, and no I will not take it off your neck for you." Twelve answered before Nargrader could ask him to remove the cut.

There was a loud noise 10 miles away that came from the town in the west.

"Time to go and save another town from disaster!" SnakeWolfe and Twelve shouted at the same time.

(If we can handle the trouble, no matter what it may be, then nothing will stand in our way. It will be just the three of us, so I hope that we won't have to much trouble. I have faith that as a team we won't have to many problems.) Twelve thought to himself having some doubts.

Twelve was worried about what they could not handle. If they couldn't handle anything what would they be able to handle. The three of them already knew each other from and by the heart which is why they became such great friends right away.

Chapter 5
TRIP TO ANOTHER NEW TOWN

The three of them were camping in the woods and having a great time. They were laughing at jokes they were telling stories and having a blast. Twelve put out the fire and SnakeWolfe stayed up all night. When Twelve woke up SnakeWolfe was holding a man with his arms behind his back.

"I found him following us so I brought him to you." SnakeWolfe said while tightening his grip because the man tried to get free.

Twelve examined the man and realized that he was scared.

"What is your name?" Twelve asked with a blank look on his face.

The man hesitated to answer for a few seconds and then he answered the question.

"my name is Joeker sir and I did not mean any harm." Joker said still a little scared, but less so because SnakeWolfe let him go.

"Joeker, may I shake your hand please? Twelve asked extending his hand out to him.

Joeker and Twelve shook hands. Twelve saw his past and he saw a little evil in his heart.

"Joeker, what did you do in your life that was an evil deed? I apologize but I see the past whenever I shake hands with someone." Twelve said while trying not to get upset that he saw that in Joeker's past.

"It's all right Twelve I understand where your coming from. I Joeker will tell you what I did. I killed my closest friend in his sleep. I am now on a journey to get rid of the evil in my heart. The journey that I've been on, I've been on for five years now. I'm traveling to the next town. This town is called the town of Dragon-Seers. Which is the town we are heading to." Joeker explained, afterwards he took a drink of water from his canteen

Sarus went to get food by herself. She walked about a mile and looked around. She waited five minutes and an Agra-mental came forth out from behind the trees that were in front of her. These creatures are random attackers. Sarus' attack is not that powerful because she is just a baby so she has to attack by biting and wiping her tail at her opponent The Agra-mental is a very powerful creature and when killed it gives off 500 pounds of dust. Every time she attacks, she hits about ten times because she is fast. She attacked first and the Agra-mental was surprised. Sarus attacked again and won. She grew two more feet. After the battle was over she roared a victory roar, and her roar also let the others know where she was so that the dust could be collected. After she got done hunting she brought back an ugly looking creature called Groogana. They ate in peace until a mysterious voice called out in the night.

"I know what you are here for and it is pointless to try to kill an Immortal unless you are an Immortal." The voice whispered in a his like a snake that could send chills down your spine.

"Who are you and what do you want with us?" Twelve asked while trying to find who ever it was.

"I'm the one you've been after, I'm the darkness that swallows the light, the nightmare that eats nightmares, I'm the evil that makes other evil run away, I'm that which disturbs your deepest and darkest thoughts. My name is Nightmare." Nightmare said with a dark aura that surrounded him.

He walked out from behind a bush. He had completely red glowing eyes. If you looked directly into them you would be overwhelmed with fear. So much so that it would be paralyzing. He was wearing a black cloak that covered his face. If you could see his face you would be brought to your knees from the intentness that radiates from it. If you stared at his face long enough you would see your death happen right before your eyes, but still be kneeling right where you were. You would eventually start begging for Nightmare to kill you. If his body wasn't hidden by the cloak, you would see that in truth he doesn't actually have one. if he did not have the cloak on all that would be there is his head, neck, shoulders, and arms floating in midair.

"I will give you a clue on how to become immortal, you have to kill your brother or your father, or even a friend that is extremely close to you and drink from the Spring of Immortality, which I think is disgusting." Nightmare said throwing up before he disappeared into the night.

He left the area leaving a couple of creatures such as an Anglishias and a Ronosorus. An Anglishias looks like an angle fish with lots of poisonous spikes on four legs A Ronosorus looks like a brontosaurus with pointy teeth and a rhino without a horn. The Ronosorus attacked first and SnakeWolfe did an attack using his anger. He killed Ronosorus in one hit then he ran to the Anglishias, jumped on its back and stabbed straight down into a hole in the middle of its back. SnakeWolfe then threw his swords into a nearby tree cutting it in half up and down, lifting it up from the ground, he turned it into firewood in the same moment. They packed up their stuff and started heading to town. When they got there, they heard an explosion nearby and went to investigate.

The explosion was from a little man called a Dragon-Seer. Dragon-Seers are the colony of people who live in the town called Dragon-Seers. They are short like a dwarf, make weapons the same way elves do when they make theirs and they love war and their shields are made with dwarf metal, which lasts forever. They found where the explosions were coming from. The explosions were from a Dragon-Seer named Draggo. Joeker knew him right away.

"Draggo how is it going? I haven't seen you since the last time you were in my village!" Joeker asked with a huge smile on his face that would make anyone smile back right away.

"I have been developing a new weapon." Draggo answered while giving Joeker a hug.

"What is this new weapon?" Joeker asked with the same huge smile on his face as before.

The reason Joeker was smiling like that was because for him, Draggo was the closest thing he had to a brother.

"They are called Dragon Bombs, and they make this huge crater. What you have to do is light the fuse and then walk away, you have to get pretty faraway because each bomb has a five-hundred foot reach for the blast radios. That's also why the fuse is so long, they give you about two minutes to get away before the bomb goes off." Draggo said with a hint of warning in his voice while explaining how the bombs work.

They stepped forward ten more steps and there was a rustling sound in the woods. A

Snake-Ragnagrieosh and a La-Greasha jumped out of the woods. A Snake-Ragnagrieosh is a giant snake that is very poisonous. A La-Greasha is a giant lion which has a poisonous acid in it's bite. SnakeWolfe took out his swords but was to slow. The Snake-Ragnagrieosh and the La-Greasha bit SnakeWolfe on the neck in the same spot. Joeker killed them both at the same time. Draggo was shocked. He called the other Dragon-Seers to open the gate. Twelve picked SnakeWolfe up and brought him inside. He told Sarus to stay outside and stop any monsters from trying to get into the town. She nodded her heads. When the gate closed Twelve brought SnakeWolfe into the nearest house and set him on a bed so they could help SnakeWolfe.

"Draggwina I need you to come check out this bite on SnakeWolfe's neck." Draggo asked while Twelve set him onto the bed.

They all let Draggo's wife, attend to him.

"How much time does he have Draggwina?" Twelve asked when he saw the look of sadness on her face.

"He doesn't have very long, maybe an hour." Draggwina answered walking away upset that there was nothing she could do.

Joeker stepped forward.

"What is it Joeker?" Draggwina asked, with a little bit of hope in her eyes when she saw the look on his face. (I haven't seen the look of determination in a thousand years, Joeker must believe that he can save SnakeWolfe's life.)

"He doesn't have to die. I can bite him and he will live. But he will become the SnakeWolfe of legend The legend goes like this, many centuries ago there was a child named SnakeWolfe, he was extraordinarily powerful, so powerful that he could have destroyed the world. However, because SnakeWolfe loved life so much he made a promise, to never hurt anyone with his power. One day SnakeWolfe was playing outside with the animals and some friends until a huge storm came. He went to his home, to watch the news with his parents. (This storm looks like the storm of the century) At that moment SnakeWolfe went back outside, it was hailing and raining, the wind was blowing very fast, and there were tornadoes, and thunder and lightning all over the place. He saw a little girl standing a block away from him, he went to her and brought her home. The girl's mother shouted over the storm. They've named this storm after you because of how much power you have.) He looked at her and smiled, then he started walking to the top of the hill that was just outside the village. He made this declaration; My name will live on forever never ending, my name is no longer a name that means power, no, it shall now be a name that represents and means protector; after that he dug deep into his heart searching for all of the emotions that he's ever had, all of the feelings that he's ever experienced. When he did that he transformed, and then he jumped into the eye of SnakeWolfe and unleashed all of his power. In doing so he sacrificed himself to save the home and the people he loved." This was the reason I was ready to join you. You see I had a vision that showed me that I would save a man who wasn't a man but a child at the age of six. His power was unlimited because of his anger welding up inside him. Joeker replied in an explaining tone.

Joeker bent down and bit SnakeWolfe on the neck in the same spot that the two creatures did and then he stepped out of the room. Twelve followed him and saw Joeker having a seizure and then a flash of bright blood red light came from his body. This red light was caused because Joeker's body was absorbing the poison that came from SnakeWolfe's body. While writhing in pain he manged to shout something.

"I have to drink from the spring or I will die in a half hour!" Joeker shouted.

Draggo showed him where it was. While still having the seizure he manged to get up off of the ground long enough to drink a handful of immortality, and a flash of white light came from him this time. Draggo thought Twelve was there to drink to and moved out of the way. Twelve told him about what Nightmare said.

Draggo just stood where he was and did not say anything; he just stood there and pointed to Twelve and then the spring. Twelve went to the spring and drank a handful of immortality when he drank it his sword flew straight up in the air and landed in the spring. When he pulled, his sword out of the spring he had realized that he was different. He became Twelveontia the Twelve that saved the world the first time. When there was a noise in the background, everyone turned around. SnakeWolfe walked out of the house. He was walking toward Twelve and Joeker, and then stopped walking abruptly when he saw the letter. The letter that was in Draggo's hand. A boy had just dropped it off. Five minutes before SnakeWolfe woke up. It was from SnakeWolfe's aunt Nerana. He ran forward and snatched it from him. The letter said:

Dear nephew

I have to tell you something that is very disturbing and hard to talk about. Two creatures attacked your mother that I did not know how to kill. The creatures caught me off guard. We were in the garden outside the town. I wrote this letter in my dying breath.

SnakeWolfe dropped the letter and started yelling. In fact, he yelled so loud that the earth cracked beneath his feet and he started floating in the air. His skin became a dark blue with spikes growing on his arms and legs. His back started cracking as he grew a few feet and his spine started to narrow. The last thing that happened was that he grew a tail that was black with a shiny silver line down the middle. He turned around and jumped over the wall realizing that the two creatures that attacked them were the same that killed his mother with twelve on his tail almost literally they went looking for those creatures, the two that Joeker killed were only the babies, but that didn't make a difference to SnakeWolfe. Draggo walked over to the letter and picked it up to throw it away when he realized that it was written in his aunt's blood, she must have held on just long enough to to drag herself to the nearest house, asking them to send the letter to SnakeWolfe.

Chapter 6
THE HUNT

They were in the trees, jumping from tree to tree. Twelve was doing everything in his power to keep up but he was still a little too slow. They fallowed the tracks that lead the way to the creatures that were going to attack the town. They found the two creatures with Nightmare waiting for them.

"The two creatures are mine!" SnakeWolfe shouted.

It sent chills down Twelve's spine causing him to shake but none the less he jumped up in the air with his sword in his hand and hit Nightmare on the arm cutting it off. Nightmare was gone in a flash. Twelve turned around to help SnakeWolfe but he won his battle. They started going back when they heard pounding on the ground. It came from the left of them. They went to the sound and they found two creatures fighting on the ground. The first creature was an Agrognia and the other was a Gore-Gonea. The Agrognia is a Werewolf that can change at will and this one was a female. The Gore-Gonea is a very powerful creature and it is a giant worm. A night crawler that we pick out of the ground or buy from a store to go fishing in real life is what she was fighting. SnakeWolfe started walking forward and Twelve stopped him. They both sat on the ground and watched the ongoing battle.

The Agrognia ducked and clawed the under belly of the Gore-Gonea and it wrapped around her and started squeezing.

"Is that the best you can do? On the other hand, do you think you can do better than that Meknagrea?" SnakeWolfe asked in a friendly and yet mocking way, trying to be funny.

Meknagrea looked in his direction. She relaxed her body and then opened her arms like there was nothing holding her in place. She then did an upper cut into the Gore-Gonea and it died.

"Good work Meknagrea, you won your first battle." SnakeWolfe said with a laughing smirk on his face.

"That's not my first battle and you know it SnakeWolfe." Meknagrea said giving a laughing smirk back.

Twelve just sat there with the look of confusion.

"Oh, I am sorry Meknagrea you must morph into your human form, so Twelve can hear you." SnakeWolfe said, now laughing at Twelve.

"I cannot morph because the Gore-Gonea attacked me from behind catching me off guard, causing me to morph in an uncontrolled manner." Meknagrea told him, with a smile.

SnakeWolfe pointed to her and then the bushes, took a pair of his sweat pants and one of his shirts, and gave them to her. He always wore two sets of clothes, two shirts and two pants. She got lucky because he had put the sweat pants on over his pants during the camp cleanup before they got to the town. She understood and went to change and came back. Then SnakeWolfe asked her if she was pregnant and she said yes. By this time, SnakeWolfe had calmed down and Twelve had started to relax. They went back to the town and saw a terrible sight.

Meknagrea was so mad that she took the clothes that Twelve gave her off and she morphed. They looked for survivors and found none. They came across Joeker while he was pulling himself together. Meknagrea picked him up with one arm and shook him.

"Put me down you witch or I will stab you." Joeker threatened grabbing his sword and pointing it at her heart.

"You are the one that killed my husband you little fatherless brat!" Meknagrea shouted in anger.

At that moment, Joeker stabbed her straight through her heart. She pulled the sword out and cut his head off. She healed instantly because her kinds are immortals of the old ones, which gives her, her healing power. He caught his head and he set it back on to attach it with a loud pop. Twelve jumped in between them and caught the swords. When he did that, they stopped fighting.

"Joeker how could you, and how dare you attack her, she is a very important person who has to be alive for SnakeWolfe's future. You have no right to attack a pregnant woman. You have to protect your sister with your life. She is a very important key to SnakeWolfe's survival." Twelve asked holding back his anger. Surprised that he would attack a woman.

"Please forgive me my lord, for I did not know she was pregnant. I also apologize to you my deer sister, I shall help you protect your unborn child." Joeker said in a sincere and apologetic voice.

They heard a roar that caused the house they were standing next to, to fall down and they went to it to see what it was. Sarus was battling against two of her kind. Twelve automatically took out his sword and jumped the remaining 100 feet landing right in front of the second Sarus. He swung his sword and stopped when he saw them kneeling in front of him. The second one spoke in an angry voice.

"Twelve, my lord I am sorry about attacking the town." The Sarus apologized, while bowing his head.

"You should be sorry, you killed all of my friends and now, now you expect me to except your apology!" Twelve shouted in an extremely angry voice.

"No, I expect you to kill me for my irresponsibility. Say something Nogronak-Mogreum, to show the respect he dissevers" The second Sarus said, grabbing the first Saurs' head and forcing him to bow.

The first one burst out into tears and apologized for his actions. Twelve threw his sword up into the air and it landed in the ground an inch from Nogronak-Mogreum's nose.

"Pick it up and kill me with my own sword and I will forgive you both for what you did but if you do not then I will kill you instead for your insubordination on this town." Twelve said, with a grin on his face.

Nogronak-Mogreum stood up and picked up the sword and cut up, down, left, and right. Twelve grabbed his sword with a grin on his face and fell apart. They both ran away and never attacked a town ever again. Twelve just finished putting himself together. When he stood up, he said they must have been scared when they saw me putting myself together and because of the pop when the bones started connecting together. Twelve ran around in a circle around each building putting out the fires on each one as he caused a little twister. They started rebuilding the buildings and finished each house within five minutes. The day was half-gone and they slept the rest of it and the night.

Chapter 7

THE NEXT DAY

When they woke up Twelve said hi to SnakeWolfe and was surprised to see all the Dragon-Seers were all back in the town. He then remembered that they were all immortal as well. The four of them left the town knowing they had a very long journey ahead of them. What they did not know was that the monsters were going to get tougher and territorial because they wouldn't want them to be in there territory. Only four left because Sarus wanted to protect the town so she stayed behind. The Seers did not think it was necessary but they thanked her any way. They started walking towards the next town, which was about 100 miles away.

The name of that town was the Town of Future. In that town people go there to look at their future when they are not sure of it themselves. When they feel strong enough to handle the information, because sometimes knowing your future is a very powerful amount of knowledge. That is if they can handle seeing their future. That is if they can handle their future. The people that live there are like Twelve, only they see the future instead of the past. They stopped at an inn 10 miles out and spent the night. Once again, SnakeWolfe staid up the whole night thinking that we were going to end up attacked by the enemy. Twelve told him that he was worrying too much. When he woke up SnakeWolfe was in the middle of a battle with Meknagrea.

"What are you two doing?" Twelve asked, with a very confused look on his face.

"We are preparing for the battle that awaits us outside." Meknagrea answered.

"What battle are you talking about?" Twelve asked, still trying to understand what was going on.

"Look outside, through the window and see for yourself with your own eyes." Both SnakeWolfe and Meknagrea answered simultaneously.

Twelve walked to the closest window and saw five hundred monsters that he never saw before. He was so shocked his jaw dropped. The creatures were an Oreg-Bogon, a Dro-Kong-King, a Spike-Ballgronkea, a giant Hog-Ganesha, a Tigrashija, Yuck Ma-Hester, and many more. An Oreg-Bogon is huge creature, it's like a snake on two legs, the only difference, is that they can eat everything and anything, no matter what it is. They don't care about anything. Drokongking's are usually very peaceful, but once you use magic on them watch out because they go berserk. They are basically a Gorilla on steroids.

A Spike-Ballgronkea is a ball with spikes that it shoots outward whenever it wants to and they grow back, instantly. They are usually more dangerous when in water but while on land they are usually slow, except their spikes. A giant Hog-Ganesha is a Boar only it's as big as a car and it has tusks like an elephant. It will eat anything smaller then it is, even it's own babies if they don't leave the nest, after they are born. Tigershija's are saber tooth cats with black fur. They are one of the fastest creatures in the world. Unlike the Hog-Ganesha, the Tigrashija care's for it's babies. Yuck Ma-Hoster is a giant spider with 16 legs

Twelve grabbed his sword and waited for the others. SnakeWolfe was already ready to fight, and Meknagrea was to.

"I do not want you to fight in your condition Meknagrea." Twelve said while holding her back.

"Nevertheless, you need my help in this battle." Meknagrea protested with excitement in her voice.

"I agree with anything Twelve says." SnakeWolfe said, doing stretches to make sure he was ready to go out there to have some fun.

"Yeah I to agree with Twelve, but I agree because you hold SnakeWolfe's savior." Joeker said, giving her a hug to make her feel better.

"Fine but what should I do if I cannot fight, Meknagrea tossed out there." Throwing her arms around her waist as if she was trying to make a point.

Before they could answer her there was a man calling from the crowed.

"Meknagrea! I know you're here." The man yelled out, getting everyone's attention.

"I recognize that voice, I would recognize it from anywhere." Meknagrea said with some force in her voice that made her sound angry. It is my ex-husband.

Joeker started getting upset and just about lunged out of the window, but Twelve stopped him.

"What do you want from us and why?" Twelve asked, while holding back his frustration.

"I want the woman and no one will get hurt I promise." The man said without a satisfying and comfortable voice.

"His promise is worthless, you cannot trust him at all." Meknagrea said, proving Twelve's suspicions about the man.

"What is your name mystery and unforgivable traveler?" Twelve asked with the question sticking in his throat a little more then he had hoped.

"My name is Hujackalag-Nogreana and I will send the monsters away when I have the woman whose name is Meknagrea." Hujackalag-Nogreana said with his fingers crossed behind his back.

"Send the monsters away first and you can have Meknagrea." Twelve said also crossing his fingers behind his back.

"I agree and I am sending them away now." Hujackalag-Nogreana said while waving for the monsters to back away. (I'll stop them right now while they are just behind the tree line. Now as soon as I get Meknagrea I'll send them to attack.)

The four of them jumped out the window after the monsters were gone with a loud thud when SnakeWolfe and Joeker had landed causing a crater you could tell that they were in a very bad mood and would have killed Hujackalag-Nogreana on sight if they did not trust Twelve to do it for them. When they got to Hujackalag-Nogreana, he grabbed Meknagrea on the arm and cut twelve in half at the same time Twelve cut his head off and it landed on the ground. The monsters were on them but stopped when they saw SnakeWolfe and Joeker. They turned around and went back to their homes. SnakeWolfe and Joeker turned back and Twelve popped himself back together again, then they left the inn and continued their journey.

Chapter 8

RUINS AND NEW POWER

"Hey, where are we going Twelve, I've never seen this patch of woods before?" Joeker asked, while looking at all of the pretty flowers and trees with flowers blooming all around them.

"We are going to a place I remember from my past life that resides here in this forest. A secret place that I used to hang out by myself when I was coming up with spells." Twelve explained with a smile, now that his body started merging with his past.

"Oh." Joeker said in surprise, with Twelve's answer.

When they stopped, they were at this cave and Twelve went inside holding his hand out to stop them from following him in. He pulled his sword out and walked forward. When he reached the end of the cave, what he saw was ruins.

"(My home was destroyed and by the looks of it, it had been since I last lived here.) I cannot believe how much it has changed since the last time I lived in this place. Now all it is, is a disaster, half of my stuff is gone and all my scrolls with my spells on them." Twelve said in his head and then out loud.

There was a grumble from under all the rubble. Twelve went straight toward the sound and noticed he was unable to remove the rubble without cutting it out of the way. Twelve did not want to hurt anyone on the way so he ripped the wood away by hand which was a lot harder, and it took him longer. When he finished there was a man that he did not recognize.

"Are you alright?" Twelve asked helping the man stand up.

"I am fine but I am surprised that you knew where this place was, who are you and how did you know about this place?" The man asked.

"My name is Twelve and I came here from the human world, who are you?" Twelve asked in return.

Twelve built a fire and cooked some food and they ate in silence. His friends camped outside until morning. When Twelve woke up the man was awake and finally answered Twelve's question.

"I am one of five gods and my name is Metrogna." Metrogna answered with a smile.

"you, are one of the gods that created this world are you not?" Twelve asked, hoping that he would hear a yes to his question.

"Yes I am and I waited for you to come here because I have a test for you to pass." Metrogna said, said while finishing his breakfast.

"What is this test and how do I pass it?" Twelve asked rubbing his hands together to get the crumbs of bread off of his hands.

"You must beat me and a Kenworthong-Agroager. The Kenworthong-Agroager is going to be under my control and how you have to find out yourself. Your friends cannot help you, you must do it on your own and this test is to prove your strength in your physical attacks." Metrogna said while putting the fire out.

Twelve took his sword out and waited for the test to start but before it started Metrogna teleported, them to a dimension called Gorgonzola battlefield. This field is where things do not use gravity but elements to fight in battles.

"Metrogna how am I going to beat you, you're a god?" Twelve exasperated, because he had a little bit of fear in his mind.

"I won't use my god powers in the battle." Metrogna answered with a smile.

Right then the Kenworthong-Agroager attacked. Twelve was knocked down to the field and got up again this time he was ready to be attacked but this time Kenworthong-Agroager and Metrogna attacked at the same time. When they attacked, Twelve did not act at all; his sword just raised itself and blocked the attack on its own. Twelve became one with his sword, which has not ever been done before ever in any history. This is called Gwone with the sword.

"I am surprised that you have done this." Metrogna said while trying to strike a blow to Twelve's head.

The battle continued and Metrogna and Kenworthong-Agroager kept attacking, attack after attack. Twelve finally started attacking back. First, he cut off the leg of Kenworthong-Agroager and Metrogna heeled the creature, which stalled Metrogna, and Twelve killed him. He had to kill the creature now in order to pass his test so he went back into regular fighting mode. He dodged the next attack and did his slice attack cutting the Kenworthong-Agroager in pieces, the battle was over and they were back on earth.

"You are an excellent fighter and very strong, in fact you are stronger then the original Twelveontia that used to live in this cave."

After Metrogna said those words he became a ball and went into Twelve's body and Twelve absorbed the power from Metrogna. After an hour, the orb hung from a necklace that magically appeared around his neck. Twelve walked out of the cave and the entrance to the cave, caved in never to be lived in again by anybody. His friends were waiting for him with their swords out. There were two creatures outside the cave and Twelve motioned his friends to put their swords away, and there claws. Twelve took out his sword and Twelve took a step without his body moving from his spot and killed the two unknown creatures. With his new power, he was so fast that one-step he took, would take his spirit one hundred steps to catch up with his body. His friend's jaws were wide open with astonishment.

"That's amazing." They all said at the same time, in stereo.

"Thank you, very much I am glad you guys are proud of me." Twelve said patting himself on the back.

They headed to the next town, which was five hundred miles away.

"This town is Geagle, by the Geagle gods of ancient past this town was made. These gods gave the people the power to live in the air. There houses literally float 50 miles in the air." Twelve said while skipping because he was so happy.

"Fifty miles in the air, are you serious, come on Twelve you are kidding right? Joeker asked in disbelief

"Nope I'm not kidding Joeker." Twelve answered, admiring Joeker's reaction.

"How do you expect us to get up in their town?" Joeker asked kind of wondering whether or not they would have to sleep on the ground while they were there.

"I have a friend named Ukoga, she can fly us into the town" Twelve answered smiling really big.

They walked forward 600 feet and there was something in the bushes. Twelve went to them and there was a child laying there crying. He picked up the baby and he knew who's baby it was. He picked up his pace and the others followed him as best they could. They got to the next town and he jumped as high as he could going full speed and landed on the first house, which was actually a church.

"Twelve what do you want us to do?" Meknagrea asked in awe at how amazing Twelve had become.

"I want all you to wait right where you are because there is somebody in those bushes; I want you to capture him fore me." Twelve answered pointing in the direction of the bush that he was talking about.

"Why is he important." SnakeWolfe asked trying not to be rude about it.

"He is not important to me but he is important to someone, so please just do it." Twelve answered with patients in his voice.

"OK I will do it in my real form so that he doesn't put up a fight." SnakeWolfe said while beginning to transform

He changed and caught the man. Twelve realized what he he had to do. He ran into the church and found Ukoga inside. He was trying to sneak up on her with his new power but she sniffled and then turned around.

"Twelve how do you expect to sneak up on me when you are holding my Junior Geagle, I could smell him from a mile away?" Ukoga asked giving him a hug.

Twelve did not say anything and left the church. Ukoga followed him and brought his friends up to the town. He stayed on the ground and studied the man who was fallowing him and his friends.

"Are you in need of assistance my friend or did you want to see the Town?" Twelve asked, with a puzzled look on his face.

"I was afraid to ask you for help but I was afraid because your friend's treat you like you're a god! The man said bowing his head in respect for Twelve.

"You don't have to be afraid because I will help you, but I need to know what you need help with." Twelve said to the man in a friendly manner.

"I need someone to save my village from the Waltrogna." The man said with some tears running down his face.

"What are they and why did they attack the village?" Twelve asked trying not to be to hard on the man.

"It is a long story but I will tell you everything." The man said.

Twelve told him to wait where he stood and was back faster than the man could blink. When Twelve got back, he carried the man to the village. On their way the man told his story.

"When I was a young lad, my dad told me this story. Legend has it that the god of attacks came to our village to save us from these creatures. They are white with black eyes. They live in the mountain called Mt. Rod. The mountain has now been named Rod after the great god of attacks. He came one more time to send my father on a journey to find you. You saved us and said that the next time I come I will carry your son back to the village and they will be no more." The man said.

They had arrived at the village and the creatures weren't there yet. Twelve thought that they came out at night and asked the man to let him sleep right under the stars tonight.

When it was about sundown the creatures came down, Twelve roared very loudly. He was morphing into a monster and that frightened the creatures. He became a great monster called Signorina He can do that because of the power that he has now. He started fighting. One of the creatures came up behind him and knocked him down and then a thousand others jumped on top. Twelve started to roar one more time, jumped straight up into the air, yelled Slice of Flames, and killed all the creatures. When he landed, he did not even leave a crater in the ground. After five minutes, he changed back into himself and Rod appeared out of nowhere.

"You have come to the village just like I said you would. I am surprised because I did not think that you wanted to see me. I am called Rod, which is short for Rodgroga. I am the second of the five gods that created this world." Rod said and answered Twelve's UN asked question.

"What test do I have to do now, or have I passed it already?" Twelve asked with a raised eyebrow.

"You have one more test to accomplish with me and in that test you have to beat me in battle. I will not use my powers that I have being a god however I will use all my skills that I have to fight you and we will be fighting in a place called, Naga-Rash and in this place we can't use magic at all." Rod said while using teleportation on them.

"So what about my sword I made it like this using a spell? Will I have to use a different sword or will my spell be taken off?" Twelve asked while holding his sword Element-all in front of Rod to show him what he meant.

"You will have to use a different sword because you placed that spell on yours." Rod said, unsure of his answer.

Twelve said nothing and grabbed the other sword that he used for emergencies.

"That is odd." Rod said with a look of surprise on his face.

"What's odd Rod?" Twelve asked while looking around.

"Your sword should have gone out but it didn't, and even if it had you still wouldn't be able to use it because you put a spell on it. I need you to wait right here, because I need to talk with the other gods." Rod explained before leaving Twelve to sit and wait.

Chapter 9

THE TEMPLE OF THE FIVE BROTHERS

When Rod arrived to the temple the Four Brothers that were not defeated by Twelve started talking immediately about Twelve's sword.

"I will start this meeting my brothers with the thought of one man. Twelveontia I need you to show yourself to us and tell us what has happened." Shiggroykoy said, looking at Twelveontia.

"What is the problem my friend?" Twelveontia asked, while stepping forward.

"The problem is that we can't figure out why his sword didn't go out so we want you to confront him and beat him if you must but we need to know about that sword. We are asking you to bring it to us because if it is the sword then something is not right." Shiggroykoy said asking Twelveontia for help.

"All right if you want me to fight him earlier than I'm supposed to, I will?" Twelveontia stated in a mocking tone.

"Mind you he is a very powerful man; he is more powerful than you are even with your five thousand years of experience so watch yourself carefully." Rod said as he was leaving.

He teleport-ed himself to Twelve and looked at him.

"Twelve my name is Tom and I have been sent here by the gods and they want you to fight me. You may use that sword if you wish, but it's not going to make a difference. Tom said, while lunging at Twelve.

Twelve pulled out his sword just in time to block Tom's attack. The four brothers were watching and they came up with a conclusion.

"Tom I want you to fight with your full strength, don't hold anything back. I want to see if he comes up with another attack." Rod said standing up in his seat.

Tom did not say anything but fought with his full strength and at that moment Twelve jumped in the air and started spinning in a circle and his whole body had been engulfed in flames from his sword. When he hit Tom, he knocked him about fifty feet back. When Tom got up, he ran forward and slammed his sword on the ground causing an electromagnetic wall that caused Twelve to fly back about one-hundred feet, when he landed he said:

"That is enough I have been holding back on you Tom so now I will show you my true powers." Twelve said while grinning at Tom.

He started to change, his body became bigger, and he seemed to be changing without even thinking about it. Tom backed away because he did not know what was happening to Twelve.

"Tom he is changing into the most powerful person in the world." The shortest brother named Compute-Trega said.

"What is that? Tom asked with confusion on his face and in his voice.

"That is when you have reached your inner you. It is like being angry but being able to control your anger and that is the true Twelve standing right there in front of you." Compute-Trega said, still surprised that Twelve from earth could do that and Twelveontia couldn't even though he has five thousand years of experience.

Tom did not respond but he attacked Twelve with his most powerful move called the sword upper cut of ten. He jumped up in the air and went all over Twelve attacking him with his swords. When he was done, he won the battle or so he thought. Twelve got up, and did not notice that he dropped his sword on the ground. When he got up he jumped into the air and called out Flaming Fists of Power and beat Tom. Before Tom teleport ed back to the temple, he took Twelve's sword and brought it to the brothers. They studied it and did tests to it but it did not react to anything that they said or did, it just sat there.

They were all startled when they heard a knock on their golden gate door. It suddenly burst open, Twelve was standing there with his hand out, and the sword went flying into it. They were surprised that he got into the temple even though he was an immortal he should not have been able to open the door. Before Twelve could teleport back Rod called his name.

"Twelve wait, how did you find your way into this place?" Rod asked with a questioning look on his face.

"I decided to follow Twelveontia into the portal." Twelve said with a great big grin on his face.

"How did you know it was me Twelve?" Twelveontia asked, shocked that he had figured it out so quickly.

"The way you use a sword and how you walk and talk." Twelve explained with the same great big grin.

"I will fight you now Twelve." Rod said slamming his hand on the table.

"All right Rod let's do it." Twelve said smiling.

"So why oh why do you like to fight Twelve?" Rod asked him out of curiosity

"An old man named Yackmacknarbog asked me that question and turned out to be a Mocking-Parnassus I answered the same way I am now and that is the fact that I love to fight to save the world not to;

He did not get to finish that sentence because Nightmare cut him into pieces.

"Now that I have finally found the first Twelve I think that I will have him." Nightmare said while casting a spell.

Before anybody could say anything, he cast his spell. The name was, Phantasmagoria This spell allows the caster to absorb the strength of the person he or she casts it on. Nevertheless, after he was done putting himself, together Twelve jumped in front of Twelveontia and he took his sword out.

"You all have to leave this place and go to the secret temple. When this is done the explosion will kill us all and I can't have that I need you to live!" Twelve shouted over the noise that was being caused by blocking Nightmare's spell.

"He is right even if our god powers won't be able to keep us from dying from this explosion. We will leave you here Twelve and we are sorry that we could not help you!" Rod shouted while opening a portal.

"Don't worry about me just go now or it will be to late!" Twelve shouted loudly.

When they left, Twelve sighed in relief that they were gone. After about five minutes, he dropped his sword because he could not hold back the spell anymore and the sword fell to the ground. There was an explosion and it was real loud. It was louder than a TV on full blast to drown out kids that you don't want to hear fighting and bickering. After the explosion, Nightmare left to get his power back because the spell drained all of it. When Twelve was back together, he went back to the Town of the Geagle's.

When he got there, it was destroyed and his friends were fighting the biggest creature ever in any world. This creature was called Edgewagan-Grankranieas. These creatures look like an over sized giant turtle that could walk on its hind legs, it could destroy a city with its tail and if it was in a city in the real world it would probably destroy it by walking through it. They have red skin that is supper thick, and then there's their shell which can't be cut through by regular means, and the only way to beat it is to destroy the shell using magic.

Chapter 10

TWELVE'S DESTINIE BATTLE

Twelve started running toward the creature and at the last second, he jumped up into the air barley reaching the top of its back. He had to stab into it so he did not fall back on the ground. The creature roared and shook Twelve off of its back. When he hit the ground he started running up its tail. The creature spun around and flung him right into the town. He ran at full speed jumped exactly when he reached the edge. This time he got his sword in deep. The roar that came this time shook the whole world kind of like a mini earthquake.

"I Twelve shall kill this creature with this spell." Twelve said when he got on the creature's back.

The spell he cast is called Sword Extentionagra. When he used this spell, he cut the creature in half through its shell and its spine at the same time causing the creature to burst into flames after his sword extended long enough to do it. Rod came down to the earth and started attacking Twelve. Twelve fought back, the fight lasted for ten days, and on the final strike, Twelve won the fight and Rod became a ball just like Metrogna. Twelve now found that he could now do his coolest move, that move was called Flying Geagle. It was called that because he jumped up into the air and came down like a Geagle with its wings out for a dive. Twelve would hold his sword with his feet and when he got close; he would do a back flip in the air and kill whatever was in his path. He tipped his head back and yelled for no reason, as he just wanted to relieve some stress from his body. Him, and his friends started walking and a voice called out from behind them.

"You won't die from the hands of a god but you will die from the hands of a friend one thousand years from this day." Ukoga said, while floating in the air like someone cursed, or holding a cursed object.

When she said that, everyone's head was turned toward her, and they were surprised that she had made such a prediction Twelve walked up to her and caught her before she hit the ground.

"We are camping here for the night. Joeker, set up the tent for Ukoga, SnakeWolfe collect some firewood, were going to be staying here until sunrise, Meknagrea go get us something to eat for dinner. I'm going to stay with Ukoga until she recovers." Twelve said holding his best friend extremely gently.

The night was long, slow, Ukoga slept through the entire night. She was in a lot of pain, and she was having a very hard time staying still. Twelve stayed by her side the entire night. When the food was done they ate in silence, because they were all worried about Ukoga. When the sun finally came up they put the fire out, packed everything up, and headed out.

They were almost to town when something jumped up in the air and grabbed Ukoga from behind and ripped her in half. She screamed the most horrible scream that I ever heard in my life when I jumped around I saw a Grog running away. They are like a dwarf but they kill Geagle's for fun. I had tears in my eyes. I chased him and when I found him, I cut his head off. The last words Ukoga said were that she would now see her son again and that she loved me. When her eyes closed she was gone. When her kind die, they fade away, into a bright light that shoots straight into the sky, towards the heavens.

Twelve yelled so loudly that I nearly went def. Twelve ran off to find the rest of the creatures. When he found them, he killed them all including the children for one's mistake. When he came back, he had blood covering his whole body. He did not talk about anything with us. We walked into town and stayed at an inn.

Chapter 11
THE PORTLE TO TWELVE'S WORLD

"I can't believe all the trouble we went through just to get to this place?" Joeker asked, thinking that the Inn they were in was a dump.

"Hey who's that over there?" Meknagrea asked, pointing to a man on a hill.

Twelve looked up ran towards the open window, and jumped through, and then he started running toward the person that was standing up on the hill.

"What's wrong Twelve I mean it is just some guy on top of the hill right?" Joeker asked with concern in his voice.

"That person isn't just a person it is Nightmare and he is trying to get to my world through that portal. That portal is Rashnarga." As soon as he goes through that portal it will close." Twelve said as he was running towered it.

When the portal closed, I saw that many creatures followed him into it. I tried to open the portal back up when my friends got there but I did not have enough power. I thought that my home world would be destroyed. When I lost all hope, the last of the brothers that I had not defeated came and asked me to fight them all at once. I did not refuse the battle but I was not in the mood for it. I fought them anyway and I found myself smiling. I did an upper cut to Compute-Trega and then I cut his head off. After that I spun in the air and Shiggroykoy blocked my first attack and then my second but on the third I said:

"This is over and this move will help me win against you. Speedy Slice of Hell two, which was my favorite attack. I hit him about a thousand times and killed him." Twelve said without missing a beat.

Up next was the biggest brother of the brothers his name was God-ranger He did not fight with a sword but with his fists. Twelve had to use his fists in order to win this fight. He had a low voice that was almost a whisper.

"So Twelve what is your weakness in this world or do you not have any?" God-ranger asked while punching Twelve in the face breaking his nose.

"I do not have any weaknesses in any world accept my friends." Twelve said while dodging God-ranger's attack and landing his own.

After we did a little talking and sparring, he hit first starting the real fight. I fell backward onto my back, and it hurt. My friends wanted to help me but they could not do anything because this was my final test. I did not fight back at first but then after the hundredth time he punched me in the

28

face I reacted to the hundredth one and blocked it. He had the biggest grin on his face and I did to. We fought for the longest time ever.

"How long did you fight for daddy?" his ten year old daughter Areyana asked, while jumping up and down from the excitement.

Well my little Areyana we fought for ten days and it was tiring because we did not take a break. We kept on fighting for all ten days. In the last hour, towards the end of the tenth day we hit each other with one last blow and he died. I thought that he would be the one to say something but none of them did and then I realized that I still had to fight Twelveontia once more.

I wanted to end all the battles so I took a running start and jumped into the air and I started to spin around in a circle. My body started on fire and the flame was different this time as if the sword was guiding me through my attack. When I landed, I had killed Twelveontia before he could do anything but blink. The brothers all turned into the balls and I felt there power immediately but when Twelveontia had to become the ball he absorbed them all and then became one orb.

When Twelve absorbed the orb, he became a lot more powerful He got a lot taller than the first Twelve was when he was full grown. His muscles became bigger and he was a lot stronger than the first Twelve. He was so fast it was unbelievable because you could not see him when he ran or walked. He was faster than flash he was faster than the fastest superhero ever thought about was. He is stronger than any superhero that anybody has ever thought could be. He opened the portal to get to his world and then he and his friends went through the portal. What they saw almost caused their hearts to explode on the spot.

When they got out of the portal twelve was enraged because everything was in ruins. When they looked up, they saw a castle ten miles away from where they were standing. The reason that everything was in ruins was because when Nightmare opened the portal for as long as he did, it caused everything to lose life, which caused everything to decay, and crumble, because it all became super old, super quickly.

Chapter 12

THE FIRST MILE OF TEN

The first step they took, a sword fell from the sky and landed a mile away. As if, someone told them to, the creatures in that area started to guard and protect the sword. These monsters were different because when Twelve looked in the middle he saw somebody standing in the middle of the circle where it landed. Twelve started walking towards that area. Monsters kept on attacking Twelve but he did not have to lift a finger to kill them. The man in the middle was killing them so he could test one of his friends to give them strength.

After walking a half-smile, a Rainbow giant came up to us waved his hand for us to follow him.

"You must follow me right away, I'll lead you to Lord Scratishgar, by the way, my name is Rain." Rain said as he started walking away.

"I recognize that name, yes, yes it has to be, I know who that is. I can't believe it, he's been a god this whole time." Meknagrea said with a look of realization on her face.

"Then who is it?" Twelve asked while looking at her.

"That man in that circle is Lord Scratishgar and he is the wielder of the legendary sword of Authentic-Untaga" Meknagrea said, answering his question.

As soon as they started following Rain, it didn't take them long to get to the circle, because Rain was swinging his club at every single monster, that tried attacking them. As soon as they got within ear shot, Scratishgar started talking immediately.

"Welcome back to the real world Twelve, I'm sorry that it's such a mess." Scratishgar said with the biggest grin he ever had in his life on his face.

"My lord I have heard stories but did not believe them however now I do and it feels great to know you exist." Joeker and SnakeWolfe said at the same time.

The sword in Scratishgar's hands was vibrating and he let it go. It flew right to Twelve's out stretched hand and he accepted it with love in his heart.

"I must give the five of you a test and the first one is Ukoga. Ukoga step forward if you would please." Lord Scratishgar said with a confused look on his face when she did not step forward.

"S-sh-sh-she is dead because I could not reach her in enough time to protect her when she got grabbed by the Gorg Twelve said with tears running down his face.

He could not hold it back any longer without tearing himself apart. He let it all out and yelled:
AHHHHHHHHHHHHHHHHHHHHHHHHHHHHHHHHHHHHHHHHHHHHHHHH!

When he finished he collapsed out of breath. He was still crying, uncontrollably, he even started to gag on his tears.

"I … understand that she was a great friend and I am sorry." Scratishgar said holding his head down.

"It is not your fault Twelve, you just happened to turn around to talk to us and then she screamed and died, you shouldn't blame yourself for that. She would not want you to be mad at yourself Meknagrea said, while trying to hold back her own tears.

"How would you know you only lost your husband and not the closest friend to your heart, she was like a sister to me, you know nothing?" Twelve shouted his question with venom in his words, lashing out at her.

"It is true that I have only lost my husband, but I moved on so my heart could be lifted. See if you dwell on the things that have happened then the world will not be so adventurous when you have all your other friends to support you. Ukoga died but she died for a great cause. I know your upset but you must let go because, because:

"Because she wanted you to use your anger to win this one last battle that is ahead of all of you." Lord Scratishgar said with a straight face.

Lord Scratishgar finished for her because she was lost for words. She was crying and Jocker was trying to comfort her.

"I SnakeWolfe have something to say to you Twelve, you can let something like this eat you alive on the inside but when you think about what has happened you will learn to let it go. It is just a feeling of guilt that has washed upon your shore and has made it wet. You have to dry your shore once more and you will be whole, again.

Twelve stood on his feet and thought happy thoughts.

"Meknagrea I will teach you first because in my book it's ladies first and men last." Lord Scratishgar said with satisfaction in his voice.

Meknagrea stepped forward and placed her hand in his and they disappeared.

"Did you know where they went daddy? Areyana asked with a smile on her face.

No I do not know where they went and I didn't need to know. I did not need to know because it was none of my business to know. After she came back, she was holding her daughter Agrognia because she knew she would not live after giving up her immortality to her daughter.

SnakeWolfe was next and he did the same thing that Meknagrea did by putting his hand in Lord's palm. They disappeared his test took him longer because he had to master his true form somehow, but when he came back he did not look any different.

I might not have looked different but I was a lot stronger than before. Areyana gave SnakeWolfe a dirty look and he did not speak again.

Hahahaahah I cannot believe you cowered away from my daughter. I think that, that's the funniest thing ever. Back to the story, like SnakeWolfe said before it is true he was more powerful and I could sense it.

Joeker was out of his mind, he was afraid because he did not fight much and he was shaking horribly. I could smell his fear and it surprised me that he did not get teleport ed to take his lesson. Instead, Scratishgar whispered in his ear. (You have learned the lesson I was supposed to teach you so I do not have to).

"You must camp hear for the night for the first mile was the easiest. But trust me the rest of the miles are going to get harder as you go along and get farther and farther on your journey." Scratishgar said while smiling.

They set up camp and got ready for the night. When Joeker woke up to go to the bathroom SnakeWolfe scared him half to death with a bang on one of our frying pans. He spun around and saw SnakeWolfe sitting on a log pretending to be asleep. What he was doing was thinking about something other than scaring people half to death, these are his thoughts: (I think the last thing that we will do together will cause the world to come back to normal and we will disappear into the world we came from. Which will make it look like we never existed.)

They started walking forward After they were all packed up. Half a mile before they got to their destination, SnakeWolfe suddenly stopped walking and jumped into the air and said:

"Twelve I need you to set up a protective barrier. There are mines setup around here everywhere. You must protect them all because I don't think that I will live at all. I know that I'm immortal but I think I might actually truly one hundred percent die. So farewell my friends, my family. SnakeWolfe said while charging himself up like an explosive device

Twelve put a protective shield around them and when SnakeWolfe landed, he said Xplosiv, and then the explosion killed him entirely except that he started putting himself together; when all of his bones were reconnected the popping sound was unbearable.

"How did you find the bombs. Meknagrea asked with a nice twitch in her eye.

"It was easy because I could smell them immediately. All of the bombs have a distinct smell to them." SnakeWolfe answered with a smile on his face.

They started to walk forward when Twelve started to move first when they got fifty feet from the spot they were supposed to go and a Se-crag came and stood in their way. These creatures are a huge pain because they feed off of the sad thoughts of others. Not current thoughts but the ones hidden deep within your mind. They don't attack you but they will hurt you mentally when they start sucking your inner sadness out of your mind. The sadness causes them to back away if the thoughts are horribly sad; this creature looked directly at Twelve and didn't back away but stood its ground.

I suddenly smiled and said thanks to the creature because it showed me that the only thing I needed to think about right now was to defeat Nightmare at and in his game. I started to control my feelings and did not cry.

"Why did the Se-crag help you father, was it because your thoughts were confused and exploding inside you? Areyana asked, a little confused.

"Yes my daughter that is the reason why exactly, now back to the story." Twelve said with a little laughter at the same time.

When the creature left, we all started walking forward again because it felt safe in our hearts to move forward once more.

When they reached the man in the middle no one knew who the Lord was that stood in front of them.

"Are you the next Lord or are you just a man pretending to be a Lord?" SnakeWolfe asked in a very rude way.

"Yes I am the next Lord and my name is Lord Ednogreashin. I know my name sounds evil but I promise that I am not an evil Lord. You all may call me Ed for short and now ladies first, Meknagrea." Lord Ed said with a smile.

She stepped forward and they teleport ed into a different world. When they came back it was

SnakeWolfe's turn. The same thing happened to everyone except for Joeker because he already learned his fighting lesson. It was now Twelve's turn and Lord Ed didn't teleport them to the mystery place. This time Twelve held out his sword and was struck by Thor the god of thunder and when it hit Twelve's sword a lightning bolt followed. The storm passed and as soon as it passed which was after it did its task. Twelve's power was unbelievable now and he just got more powerful after every time he saw an immortal.

Chapter 13

THE THIRD MILE OUT OF TEN

They camped for the night just like the first time. It started raining and no one asked for a shield of protection except for Meknagrea to keep Agrognia safe from harm. The reason Meknagrea asked for the protection is because it was raining because of a spell. Before they went to bed SnakeWolfe said:

"I see someone approaching the camp and they have something in there hands. Should I allow them passage or should I cut them down? SnakeWolfe Asked. Getting his sword ready.

"Let them pass, they are only here to help keep the baby safe from harm or at least that is what I can sense in their hearts Joeker said holding his hand up to stop him.

"Alright I let them pass because they promised not to cause trouble." SnakeWolfe said a little reluctantly, while grabbing another log.

He also took his sword out just in case they did cause trouble, but they set up a protective barrier around the whole camp.

"So what brings you to this part of the world friends? Joeker asked trying to start up a friendly conversation.

"We were just passing through to see what was causing it to be so bright in this area." The smallest traveler said while putting their hands next to the fire.

"It turned out to be the baby." The bigger traveler said while also putting their hands next to the fire.

"Do you know who her father was?" The little red eyed and haired traveler who took off her hooded sweatshirt?

"Yes I do, he was my brother and he was an amazing fighter. He was always remembered as the Shinning Fighter but his real name was Sonic-Hellgona, but why do you ask?" Joeker asked with curiosity

"I knew your brother very well, he was my brother in law when he married my sister, when she died, Sonic-Hellgona was devastated, a few years later he found a woman named Meknagrea. Do you know who killed him? The woman asked while looking around checking everyone out.

"Yes, I killed him. Joeker said chocking on his admittance when he answered her question.

The woman looked at him and she realized that he really did kill him when she saw the tears on his face. She stood up and jumped into the air. Joeker put his hands up to his friends and they stayed where they were. The friends of the woman didn't move because SnakeWolfe stopped them in their tracks. Before she landed she took her sword out of its sheath and started to slam her sword down where Joeker was sitting. One second almost too late Joeker had his sword in his hand and rolled out of the way. When the woman's sword hit where Joeker was sitting she got it stuck in the log he was sitting on.

Joeker put his sword back into his sheath and spun around and put her in a head lock and then asked:

"Do you want to die now or do you want to live my dear Korgonagie?"

"I want to live so that I can tear you apart because you are an insult to my family." Korgonagie said angrily.

"To bad you were so beautiful." Joeker said closing his eyes.

Before he snapped her neck she spun around and snapped his. Before he could stand back up she tried to say a magic word called Digglepieces which would cause Joeker to die. SnakeWolfe reversed the spell before she could completely say say it. Then Joeker stood up and killed Korgonagie with his strength. When he hit her he killed her in one blow and thanked SnakeWolfe for his help. The other two ran away because they were scared of them.

Agrognia started floating out of Meknagrea's arms. She floated straight to Korgonagie's body and touched it, after she touched her body. She stood up, then Agrognia said put your hooded sweat-shirt on so we don't have see that much of you and Joeker apologize to her for killing her, and then I want her to travel with us.

Everybody just stared at her in shock because she was only one and she just spoke her first sentence. After five minutes Joeker apologized and Korgonagie put her hooded sweat-shirt back on for she was wearing only a tank-top

The next day we all went on to continue our journey but then Nightmare ambushed us before we could finish packing up. He jumped up in the air and Joeker and SnakeWolfe followed suit. There was one flash of electric shock waves and power, the sky was electrified. You could have literally cooked food from the energy in the sky.

"Daddy what caused the air to become electrified?" Areyana asked, hoping that her daddy would be able to answer her question.

"Well my sweet daughter the electrons within the energy bursts caused it." Twelve answered quickly.

The three of them fought for a long time and at certain times in the battle the air would change, it would become hot, cold, freezing or time itself would stop but the battle would continue. Nightmare got the upper half of the battle and he sent SnakeWolfe crashing to the ground causing a huge crater in the ground when he landed. He was knocked out after he bounced three times. Four minutes later the same thing happened to Joeker except for half of his body was missing and he could not connect himself together again until he woke up.

"Now who wants to fight me next?" Nightmare asked with a greedy look on his face and waving his arms up and down for the next person in excitement.

"I will fight you next." Twelve answered with confidence in his voice.

Twelve sat down closed his eyes and Nightmare started laughing at him but Twelve did not do anything he stayed sitting cross-legged on the ground meditating. What Nightmare didn't notice was the dragon that was directly above him flapping its wings to stay in one place. When he stood up he whistled with two fingers in his mouth.

"Come here my beautiful golden dragon from the land of Love, hearts, prosperity, justice, and justice, come to me my dearest Oh-Halla, Twelve whispered.

Twelve's dragon's color was amazing it was so beautiful that it made a rainbow look like nothing. It gleamed in the night brighter then the moon, and there was no moon this night. Nightmare looked up into the sky wondering why it was so bright all of a sudden and then he noticed, and realized that he sat in the Dragon's Sumner's stance, this stance is when a person sits cross-legged on the ground with his arms connected in a triangle with your thumbs touching your nose.

Nightmare started laughing again and summoned his dragon as well and also so that Twelve's dragon wouldn't reach Twelve, and that's when the battle began. Twelve's Dragon against Nightmare's Dragon. Nightmare's power against Twelve's power, the battle that takes a brave heart, a battle to see who is the strongest in strength and mental strength.

"So Twelve, now we shall see who the stronger magic user is." Nightmare said while flying at him.

"I guess we will." Twelve said with a smile on his face.

The four of them fought, on the ground Twelve slashed up at Nightmare's ribs while Nightmare did the same thing. The dragons flew straight at each other head on while Oh-Halla blew flames Nygargna swallowed the flames and blew them right back.

"Use the magic within your heart Oh-Halla, it is the only thing that Nygargna is weak against." Twelve shouted with anger in his voice as Nightmare cut his right arm off, which also made Oh-Halla lose her right front leg.

Twelve cut off Nightmare's left leg and also decapitated Nightmare in a single motion. After that Nightmare called Nygargna to pick him up while he popped his head and his leg back on. He flew away and disappeared into the night. Everyone finally finished packing up their things and started heading out to the Lords circle.

When we reached the Lords circle we saw a man who looked like he was a mortal. The lord was a skinny man whose name was Auk-Known and he was an old but younger old Lord, however his power is UN-known None of us knew who he was, not even Korgonagie who was the smartest person in our group, next to Joeker.

"So who can guess the lesson that you're to learn with me today? Auk-Known asked trying not to smile to much.

"How to summon ourselves from our personal void?" Joeker asked sarcastically.

"That is correct Joeker, now how do you do that?" Auk-Known asked ignoring the sarcasm.

"I can do it myself, lord Auk-Known if you want me to do so." Twelve stated in a very relaxed tone of voice.

"Can you now? If you actually can do it, then that would be extremely interesting, would you mind showing us how to do it? Auk-Known asked, not really believing that he could.

Twelve sat on the ground cross-legged called his dragon to him and she made a circle around him. The tip of her tail was in her mouth and she had her wings unfolded, she put one over Twelve and then she put the other on the ground but then touched the tip of both wings together causing a circle of electricity to surround Twelve on the inside of the circle. He started to glow, as if he had been a piece of metal in a forge. He was red and it was strange.

Twelve started to hum a tune which called forth a storm. When the storm passed there was another huge shock wave of power that melted the clothes off of everyone. No one noticed, all they saw in that second was Twelve standing there, and Joeker walked up to him and Twelve attacked.

Joeker was caught off guard but still dueled anyway. The real twelve stood up and put his clothes on. Joeker won the duel but then Twelve stood up and went to stand next to Twelve.

"Are you happy I could do it Lord Auk-Known?" Twelve asked with a grin on his face proud of himself.

"Yes I am happy that you could do it, but how come you could is my question?" Auk-Known asked not even bothering to try and hide the fact that he was surprised.

"I can do it because the supreme high Lords of old allow me to do it my Lord. Twelve replied with a smile.

After several hours of waiting and being patient everyone learned how to summon themselves from their personal void's. They continued their journey and had an extremely good night.

Chapter 14

THE FOURTH, FIFTH, AND SIXTH MILE OUT OF TEN, THE TRIPLET LORDS

"Why haven't we just used magic to teleport ourselves to the castle and just kill Nightmare and rid the world of this darkness?" Joeker asked with ignorance in his voice.

Nobody answered him because he was drunk with unhappy thoughts because he was haunted by his inner self, he started talking to himself and he got so bad that Twelve had to put him in a coma because he started to threaten the party and himself.

"Can you help him or is the coma all that you can use to ease his pain?" Agrognia asked with concern in her voice."

"I could do a Trance-Igma, which is when I would put myself in a trance and try to enter his mind, but if I do that then I will just damage him and cause him to lose his mind. The effects would melt his brain if I made a mistake. There is one other thing that I could do and that is take him out of his coma that I put him in and then kill him after I use a special spell that will revive him afterwards but that might be even more dangerous because he might come back and kill us all, so it's a one in a million chance ether way you look at it." Twelve answered with uncertainty in his voice.

"So why don't we just revive him after we kill him and then after that, we can just explain to him the situation." Korgonagie suggested looking at everyone with a look like, do you have a better idea or what.

"We can't do that because that spell requires a sacrifice and we don't have any volunteers." Twelve said telling part of the truth.

"What kind of sacrifice is required Twelve?" Korgonagie asked.

"It requires your death and, and I know that Joeker would not want you to die, plus you have to cut yourself twenty times and, and.

"And I also have to get naked and have sex with a dead body then afterwards say the spell and then I will die, is that right? Korgonagie staged the question with loyalty in her voice because she interrupted Twelve.

"How did you know about the ritual?" Twelve asked, frustrated that she knew about it.

"I know about it because I saw one once." Korgonagie answered with tears in her eyes.

Before anyone could stop her she did the ritual and time started moving so slow you would have thought that it stopped but it didn't. It slowed down so much that every second was an hour and a minute was a day and an hour was four days and a day was a weak or longer and a month was a year or longer.

To Twelve the time in the world was already slow because of his speed, and at that time Twelve was running toward Korgonagie to stop her before she could finish the spell but it was too late. When he got to them a white glowing shield surrounded them and Twelve bounced right off of it.

When the shield was down Joeker was alive and Korgonagie was dead. When Joeker looked at the body he remembered everything and then he freaked out and fainted. When he woke up he attacked Twelve. Joeker beat on him for a long time, so long in fact that the others had to pull him off.

When they turned around they saw Agrognia walking to Korgonagie's body and she started talking to it in a language that sounded like French and Spanish mixed to equal one language. When Twelve got to her he realized that she was talking to Korgonagie through her dead body just by touching it. When Twelve reached down to remove her hand he got an electric shock that made him explode, causing one limb after another to fall off.

When she was done talking to her she touched her with her other hand and Korgonagie's body floated up in the air and landed on both of her feet with her clothes back on. Joeker ran straight at her and kissed her hoping that she would kiss him back. When she kissed him back, he felt a great serge of power go through his body causing him to shiver. Nobody asked any questions and started to leave camp.

They were almost at the circle when they started to notice that there were three Lords. Their circles overlapped which made a Mickey Mouse to equal one big circle. When the group got to the circle the three Lords stepped into the middle and then there was a flash of light that caused the group to go blind for two minutes. The Lord's were the Triplet-Gama brothers. When the Triplet-Gama brothers spoke the blindness went away and then the training began.

They were all tall, slim and extremely handsome to the women. Their hair was a cool cut, their eye color changed every one to five seconds, the color of their hair was unknown. Their lesson was about the power of love and friendship, when they were finished they gave everyone a ring and instructed them to put the ring on their middle fingers and to twist them to the left every time they heard a language they didn't understand and they also allow you to speak in that language, plus if you don't want to speak it twist the ring to the right. When they walked right past Twelve they gave him a necklace. Then they disappeared into the thin air.

Our group was half way to the next circle when Korgonagie saw the ocean and led us to it. We stopped ten feet from the shore and set up camp, after we set up camp Korgonagie picked up a bunch of rocks and started to throw them in the ocean in a particular spot, five minutes later the oldest thing in the universe, of universes including the one of the earth, came bursting out of the water. This thing is so old that it was alive far before the universe started.

This thing made a type of contract with the gods of the gods before the gods were even gods. They created this thing to protect those who would not be able to protect themselves from themselves. The gods cut a hole in its foot and collected the blood. Korgonagie woke it up and then it lay down next to her and went to sleep. It has the ability of every single fiction and nonfiction thing ever created and Mozilla's power is unimaginable. The only way you could imagine it is if you can open your mind to the Lord of imagination, who lives in space. It is definitely not something you should mess with. The odd part of this creature is that it is a vegetarian.

The Lords name was Final Saganargo and he was more powerful than Mozilla If they fought Final Saganargo would mop the floor with Mozilla even if Saganargo fought one hundred thousand nine hundred ninety-nine of them, if he fought one more then that he would have even more of a challenge then he bargained for.

He looked like a man who was short but as soon as you walk up to him he grows up to your height no matter how tall you are. His eyes were darker then darkness, and his hair was full of bugs like he started to rot from time itself, for cloths he wore only a cloth like a cave man. When he walked every bone in his body would creak like an old house that needs new floors. You could definitely tell he had been living for quite a while. Was he dead, not even close. Was he still alive, yes he was still alive when twelve and his group saw him last. All of his organs were working one hundred percent.

It was the next day when we started training. Joeker mastered a technique called Hell Rising a Hell. This technique allows him to call forth the most powerful being in hell, Cerberus. Joeker was the only one able to use this move because when he died Cerberus made a pact with Joeker. That pact was thus: I Cerberus shall save the world as long as Joeker is still alive when he reaches Nightmare's castle and I will only serve him because he has seen my true form.

I learned, I mean I mastered a technique called Hollowness. This technique allows you to become a tree monster. This tree monster is called Tregnoga. When I become Tregnoga I would cause trees to come alive and kill whatever was in front of me. Meknagrea and Agrognia were next. They had to battle each other to the death. Agrognia is like a dragon from the four book series Inheritance, the magic is in her but she does not know how to use it. She was feeling some kind of emotion both times when she helped Korgonagie come back to help us, so who knows who will win the battle.

They just stood there staring at each other, not looking at each other like they were family, no instead they looked at each other like enemies. Both determined to win the fight. Nether moved while the other stood still. If one blinked the other would flinch, and if one twitched the other would move and vice versa. This went on for so long it was too long and all of a sudden Agrognia jumped up and threw her sword at her mother, she ended up hitting Meknagrea's shield going through the steel and almost hitting her in the head. They caught their swords.

They tossed them and started the stair down once again. The Lord just stood right where he was watching every move they made. All of a sudden there was a fire blast toward the city. I thought that it was nothing and then I began to watch the girls again. Five minutes, ten minutes, a half hour, an hour, an hour and a half, and then after two hours, they finally charged each other while transforming into their real forms. While Agrognia and Meknagrea ducked it out something magical happened.

A dragon swooped down and picked up SnakeWolfe in its claws while a magical blind fold appeared on his head he said: Don't follow me just keep on training. When I tried to follow the dragon, Lord Final Saganargo reached over and grabbed me. When I looked at him he was still standing where he was which happened to be twenty feet away or more, then he said: His training is already finished, now watch as Agrognia deals the finishing blow to her mother.

When Agrognia finished her final attack delivering the final blow Meknagrea didn't die, her soul seeped out of her and floated toward Lord Final Saganargo and then stopped right in front of him and stayed floating there. The Lord motioned for Agrognia to come to him. When she came closer, the Lord started to whisper in her ear and Agrognia followed his every instruction.

Agrognia put her hands into her mother's as if she was holding her hands, but their hands became connected somehow, because her hands were the same size as her mother's they sank into them and then Lord Final Saganargo started to chant a spell that caused Agrognia to absorb the soul of Meknagrea, there was a great big flash of yellow, but gold like light that blinded all of us at the same time. When we could see again Agrognia looked one hundred times better and her power was even greater than her mother's. The last person to take on the training was Korgonagie. Her training was the shortest of all because all the Lord had to do was spar with her. She turned out to be quite the swords woman The next day SnakeWolfe was back at camp with a gray dragon whose name was Grow-Go and he was big.

Chapter 15
SNAKEWOLFE'S TALE

When we woke up in the morning SnakeWolfe started to tell us what happened. When I got taken by the dragon he landed on an island one hundred miles away and then he took me to the dragon king Grow-Go. Grow-Go wants to save mankind as long as we do not tell anyone that they exist. I told them all, that they don't have to worry. On our way back the king allowed me to contact his brain and he also showed me a way to get us to the next Lords circle. So if you want to know what happened I just told you, oh yeah Grow-go says happy dragon day.

Dragon day is when all of the dragons gather to have their young and to help save the world, and they only celebrate this day when a thousand years have passed.

They camped one last night by the ocean and the next morning they packed up their camp and then hopped on the dragon's backs, while SnakeWolfe was on Grow-go Twelve called his dragon Oh-Halla and the rest of the group hopped onto Oh-Halla's back and they followed the dragon king through his short cut. They reached the seventh Lord in five minutes and then landed in the circle. The dragons stepped out of the circle and waited outside because they were afraid of causing problems or power interference with what was going on.

The Lords name was unknown to anyone when we first met him. He spoke such a foreign language everybody had to turn their rings to understand what he was saying.

"Hi my name is Alphabet- Toga and I am to train you how to get to the last level of your abilities which is level zero. After your training is finished then the last three miles are for other things that I am unsure of, now shall we begin your training?" The Lord said with immediate command and question.

The Lord took Twelve's hand and read the lines on his palms, after that he read everyone else's palms as well. It appears that there is not a thing I can teach you after everything you have been through, so the only thing to say is that your journey is going to have a very sad ending for all of you. Beware the death in the near future of battle. After he said that he left like the other Lords and he was never heard of again.

They set up camp by a house that was destroyed from when Nightmare ended the portal the electronic waves from the portal caused a lot of damage to almost everything which is why everything looks so disconnected from the original world. When they were done setting up camp Twelve went for a walk into an area where a house was flipped upside down from an earthquake.

He sat down in a chair and closed his eyes remembering when he first came here and how he was healed from the magic of the world. How he went from being stuck in a wheelchair to being able to walk on his legs again. Looked in a mirror and saw that all of his scars were gone as well, he closed his eyes and then he saw a vision.

His vision was of a new world on earth where everybody was happy. There was no war or any fighting of any kind, the world was in a better place than it was now. The little kids were running around with smiles on their faces, and laughing because their mothers were chasing them around. The adults and parents and the teenagers were having parties and celebrating, watching movies having a night out with friends and family. Then he woke up from his vision and went back to camp.

"Twelve is something bothering you my friend, because you seem a little distracted lately?" SnakeWolfe asked with concern in his voice.

"I am having trouble wrestling with my feelings for the way things are and the way things are going to be when we stop my brother from destroying the world." Twelve answered SnakeWolfe with confusion and uncertainty in his voice.

"Well my friend the world is not for you to worry about, nope the world is only meant for you to save and allow the gods to worry about what's what in our world and yours. It is very hard to hold the weight of the world on your shoulders so just unhook your feelings from your heart and let them drift away on the wind and the stream of the invisible line of feelings that are always around to help us through our toughest times in our lives." SnakeWolfe said with a sound of comfort in his voice.

"Thank you for your advice my friend, it helps more then you can imagine, with the advice you have given me these last few months that we have been traveling together and we are like brothers and I cherish everything you tell me." Twelve said with love in his voice a smile on his face, while hugging SnakeWolfe.

After they hugged, Twelve went to sleep in his tent. When he woke up he was face to face with an animal slash creature called Ogle-Legrafana. This was a mixture with a computer screen stuck on one image and a wolf of some kind that has never been seen before. Twelve was about to attack but it held up one of its pawdaws and then grabbed Twelve by the collar of his shirt, and dragged him out of the tent. When he stood up he saw a whole pack of Ogle-Legrafana's bowing to him. They left after they all saw Twelve in front of them. When the group finished packing up there camp they finally headed off to the last three Lords one mile at a time.

We packed up the camp when the sun was full in the sky. When I looked up and saw the dragon king looking ahead to see if there was an open path without anything to slow us down in the process of reaching the circle of the Lord. He said that there were no obstacles in the way so we headed north. The dragon king took SnakeWolfe on his back and flew away to the island of the dragons. I was going to ask what was happening but decided better of it and kept on heading straight.

Chapter 16

THE TWO UNEXPECTED LORDS

While heading north we passed some buildings that were all crumpled up and then we got ambushed by these people who were sick from some kind of disease called Hammer Brainga, this disease was caused when Nightmare opened the portal too both worlds and because the two worlds were connected for the half-hour that they were. It made humans forget about the normal life that they had before Nightmare came.

"What do we do, can they be healed, will, will they be healed after all of this is finished?" Agrognia asked afraid of the answer she might get.

"Unfortunately they will never be healed, but we can end their suffering, but only if you guys choose to do so." Grow-Go spoke with uncertainty in his voice.

We lit torches and scared them all into one house, it took us about an hour to get them all in the same house and another hour to barricade the doors shut to make it so they couldn't get out, and then the king and my dragon burnt down the house. The sound was devastating and the smell was extremely unbearable. When we were all far away enough we had reached the circle of the Lord. When I saw the Lord my jaw nearly dropped off, because I recognized him immediately, I ran towards the Lord and gave him a hug.

"Dad I thought that you were dead, when I saw our house it was destroyed and your body was lying on the ground motionless. When I saw it I freaked out and had an emotional breakdown, my friends had to drag me away, I mean it made the weeks my friends and I traveled with harder than you can imagine. Seeing you here is almost heart breaking, it is just so hard, and now hear is the question that I know you are waiting for me to ask you. Is mother dead as well or did Nightmare capture her and make her his slave?" Twelve said and asked with sadness in his voice and heart because he missed his mother.

"I know that this is not easy but there is a lot that you need to know and we have so little time for you to hear it so I am going to teleport us to a place called Timeless, in this place time means nothing, if you are OK with teleporting to this place with me my son place your hand in mine?" Jack asked with a lot of unhappiness in his voice.

"What about my friends they, no I would be happy to join you father, if you guys don't mind if I spend time with my father?" Twelve asked with wondering in his voice praying that they wouldn't mind.

"We don't mind at all!" They all said with excitement in their voices, happy that he would be able to spend time with his father.

When they teleport ed to Timeless and it was a place full of indescribable beauty, if it was real and a woman saw it she would end up in the hospital for too much excitement. Twelve's dad started talking immediately and Twelve just sat there and listened.

"Twelve I'm sorry about this and hope you don't hate me for it, but first of all my real name is Seana-Roga. When you were first born it was in the world you were sent to help save the people from Nightmares tyranny in the world. The second thing is that when the five of, that's right the five of us lived in that world Nightmare didn't always go by the name of Nightmare, no your brother for he is truly your brother, well his real name back then was Joseph-Omega. Your mother named him Joseph-Omega because she saw that he was going to do something terrible but extremely great with his life. She didn't know what at the time but she still told the future somewhat. Joseph-Omega was born after you were and your, other brother well he was murdered before we could name him, and he was murdered by Joseph-Omega. That is when he started trying to learn the dark arts of magic, he was always one step behind you and decided to confront you about learning more. You refused to teach him and said that he would never benefit from your magic again. That's when you decided to hide in a cave. This cave took him several years to find. When he found it you had already prepared for his arrival and then you had a magic war, when you lost the gods sent your mother and I to planet earth and we had you and only you while we were on planet earth. It was you who showed us the reason to help the planet. So when the Lords of old contacted me I agreed to do what I had to, to help the planet which is why I am the seventh Lord that you met. After your brother killed you he took your magic and used it to try and destroy the world once before but that's when the purple orb like ball that he made consumed him. He was trapped there for 5,000 years. I suppose a man named Nargrader visited you in the hospital and told you that a man named Noxmondamon started studying the dark magic and made spells that he used to kill people, and that they were very terrible but he wanted more power, and he went to the cave that Twelveontia lived in and they started to fight, and in the end of the battle, Twelve made a prophecy that one day he would return and save everyone and that the blade of heaven would return once again to the chosen one. Well the man who visited you really was Noxmondamon and he was or still is a servant to your brother who had to, of told him to tell you that load of crap story, for it was Nightmare who did all of those things, and the reason why I said that Noxmondamon was or still is a servant is because Nightmare freed himself from his imprisonment somehow and weather Noxmondamon is still alive or not, is something we will never know, because he helped Nightmare get back on his feet somehow. The last thing I have to tell you is that before Nightmare killed me his dragon grabbed your mother and that is the last thing that I remember after I woke up in the circle of a Lord." Seana-Roga said with a load of guilt lifted off of his shoulders.

"Father I do not hate you nor should I, I have finally learned the truth of truths in my heart, you see I have always had that feeling after I met and fought Nightmare I knew that he was somehow related to us. When I fought him I could sense in his power that it was darker but the same power as mine, so now that I know the truth maybe I can save him but then again he has had this power for over 5,000 years so who knows what will happen. Joseph-Omega might be evil and call himself Nightmare but he is still my brother and I love him with my heart. I will however kill him if it is necessary. So father thank you for what you have done for me, I'm sure it will help me in the long run though." Twelve said with a happiness that he finally found deep within his heart.

They teleport ed back to the earth and then Seana-Roga asked to train Korgonagie and Agrognia at the same time so they both walked forward and he teleport ed them and himself to Timeless, to us they were only gone for a few hours but when they were in Timeless they were gone for a weak that just past in a day while in Timeless and to us on earth it was a few hours. When they got back he asked Joeker and SnakeWolfe to train with him but when Twelve walked forward Seana-Roga shook his head and said that he had learned his lesson already so Twelve stayed behind and started to help the girls set up camp when all of a sudden king of the dragons came back from a flight with food for all of us and he was also injured.

When I asked him what happened he didn't explain right away but when SnakeWolfe came back he answered the question gladly.

"I went on a hunt on SnakeWolfe's orders so we could all have supper tonight when I was ambushed by a herd of these Hogrogs. You humans probably have never heard of them but they are a type of warthog that are more vicious with larger bodies and their tusks are longer and sharper not to men chin that when they travel in a herd they are not afraid of anything once so ever. The king of the dragons answered with pain in his last words.

SnakeWolfe walked over to the king Grow-Go and whispered something in his ear and then healed his torn up leg while killing the Hogrog that still hung there and threw it up in the air for Grow-Go to eat. He caught it and thanked SnakeWolfe for his help. The sun was coming up in a couple of hours so we slept until the sun just started rising and then we packed up our gear and left for the next Lord's circle when we were half way there we were attacked by a huge herd of Rogs.

Rogs are over sized frogs with fangs like a saber tooth tiger. We were surrounded. The dragons were going to just blow their flame but SnakeWolfe and I told them not to. SnakeWolfe, Joeker and I helped the girls onto the backs of the dragons one on each dragon and then the three of us jumped in the air and performed an attack called Flaming Circle, the three of us held hands and then started chanting which caused our swords to start on fire and then we started spinning around which started to spread out the flames killing all of the Rogs in one shot.

When we reached the Lord's circle we were all surprised because it was a woman who was standing in the circle this time instead of a man. When we landed she took a walk to my dragon and hopped on. She said nothing and Agrognia jumped off. The Lord pointed to the circle and then the dragon and then the circle again and we went forward. When Oh-Halla got into the circle the Lord decided to teleport us to an unknown realm. It was all white except for the color from Oh-Halla's scales. The Lord whistled and her dragon came out of nowhere and the four of us started fighting. We started to fly and spiral in the air claws hitting claws and swords hitting swords. I would do an upper cut and then I turned the blade to cut her in half but she blocked me at the last second while my dragon used her tail to break the other dragon's ribs and break its neck but it blocked her tail to the ribs and dodged her completely which allowed the Lord's dragon to get behind us.

Her dragon bit and held onto my dragons tail and would not let go. The Lord started to attack me from behind so the only thing I could think of to do was get out of the dragon saddle and run from Oh-Halla's back and onto the other dragon but when I was going to attack the Lord yelled stop and she healed all of our wounds and all of her own wounds as well. Then she teleport ed us back to the earth and did the same with the girls and SnakeWolfe with the king's permission. After she gave each of us a lesson she pulled me aside and asked me whether or not I would be marring Agrognia and I told her that she is just a child and I am an adult. You are also a child Twelve especially in the presence of the Lords so I will tell you that she is the one and only woman for you in your life. While she started teleporting she whispered, there will be many women in your life, but you will only love Agrognia, and then she was gone.

We were almost to the circle when a strange fog as thick as bricks, I mean you could make donuts after donuts, it was endless. We got lost, even the dragons couldn't fly over the fog nor could we see them blow their flames ether. We did not know what to do so we set up camp and in what we thought was a safe spot, but when we woke up the fog had cleared, and there was some kind of giant bugs everywhere. This bug was called Flash-Fog-Grog. It has a type of gland that it uses to confuse its prey and then when their prey is confused they surround them and then attack with giant mosquito like teeth. If it needs to it will also attack you with its mind which causes you to fall down unable to move. There were thousands maybe hundreds of thousands we could not tell how many there were.

Nobody was moving afraid they would provoke the Flash-Fog-Grog into attacking them. It was absolutely crazy because off in the distance there was a sound and then they just left and went in that direction. The group packed up their things as quickly and quietly as they could and when they reached the circle, the last Lord was fighting Nightmare and Nightmare was winning.

"We have to help the Lord or we won't be able to fight Nightmare and win, but what should we do?" Agrognia shouted her question.

As if in answer the Lord cast a spell and grabbed all of us at once causing us to float to the circle and then we landed in the circle. The dragons and even our equipment all at the same time. Then the Lord spoke: Twelve, SnakeWolfe, and Joeker help me win against this Nightmare of Nightmares please? The Lord asked with a pleading voice.

All three of us jumped into the air but we didn't get more than fifty feet before we were frozen in place by a spell that Nightmare had placed. The spell was, and I say was because if this kind of spell got abused it could kill the people frozen in one spot, If they were forgotten. The spell's name was Frizganoka-Kie-kiewa. This spell was not created by any human being, it was created by a monster named Name. Name was an evil before evil itself became evil. Nobody and I mean nobody could have used this spell except for Name.

"So daddy why and how did Nightmare get the spell, unless he could travel back into the past or bring somebody back to life, which are all far fetched ideas right daddy?" Areyana asked being just a little scared of her father because of the look on his face.

"Yes you are right and I was trying to ignore those possibilities, but you are right any way and now Joeker needs to explain what happened because I, I passed out after being held for five minutes in the spell. Twelve answered with an agitated voice.

Right! what happened, well that is easy: will you get on with it already Joeker your wasting time! Areyana shouted with annoyance in her voice!"

Like I was going to say, before you interrupted me, I yelled out to Agrognia and told her to cast a counter spell because we all knew the spell that was being used against us, you see all she had to do was cast a simple spell that would put us down but Nightmare was a spell casting master like Twelve it took Korgonagie and the dragons combined strength in order to break his spell, after the spell ended I thought that Twelve would wake up, but he just fell. Before he hit the ground Oh-Halla caught him in her jaws and then set him on the ground, then she transformed into a gold Twelve and jumped up to help us. The three of us started attacking Nightmare with as much power as we could muster. With the four of us all attacking at once he fled but before he could get very far the gold Twelve threw a javelin at him and then Nightmare was gone.

We started training with the Lord right away, before any of us could recuperate after fighting Nightmare which surprised everyone because Twelve hadn't woken up yet, which scared me, he passed out in such a manner that his heart wasn't beating. It was like he was dead but he was really still alive just not moving. She said that we had to start our training immediately, so we did what she told us to do and then when she finished training all of us she walked over to Twelve, put her hands on his head and then she closed her eyes. She stayed crouched there for two hours, but when she was done she disappeared.

Chapter 17

THE FINALE MILE PART 2

For now we set up camp right here until Twelve wakes up or we will keep going, but we will sleep on it for now until morning OK everyone.

"Joeker you can shut up now! I'm sure daddy wasn't still in that coma or whatever you call it!" Areyana said very upset now and thinking that this was some kind of a joke.

"Um actually that is as far as I can tell you our journey for quite some time Areyana so I would like you to stop interrupting Joeker and let him finish, like your brother, well I mean I know you can't speak yet son but you haven't even made any sound what so ever. So I am impressed, now stay quiet like your brother or you won't hear the rest of the story." Twelve told her with a sarcastic smile on his face.

"Hey that's not fair, no fair at all Daddy! Mommy! Mommy!" Areyana cried, while throwing a fit.

What is it sweaty, I'm in the middle of cooking super? Agrognia asked while staying focused on what she was cooking.

Daddy! Won't tell me the story and Joeker isn't doing a good job of it!" Areyana complained.

"Joeker is doing a fine job honey, your just used to hearing Daddy tell you stories, now behave yourself and listen or I am going to send you to bed, and also because your Daddy was still at that time in, ahem, excuse me, in that coma for that was exactly what it was. The name that this coma goes by is, SleepComaGo and he was in it for a very long time all right. God I can't believe how chocked up I get from explaining part of my husband's history. Agrognia said in answer to Areyana's complaining.

When we were all awake I told SnakeWolfe to get everyone's attention, which he did and then I called a meeting: What do you guys think we should do, I know I am the second person to be in charge when Twelve can't speak his plans but I do not know how long this coma will last nor do any of you, we need a plan and we need one as soon as possible, so anyone have any suggestions of any kind. No, how about you SnakeWolfe, that mind of yours never stops turning it's gears maybe you can give us a plan I mean since you have an ability to stay up night after night without sleep of any kind, maybe I should pass the leadership off to you. What is thy opinion? Joeker asked with question in his voice the whole time he spoke.

Before SnakeWolfe could voice his opinion Nightmare appeared in front of them but he didn't attack or anything, he just spoke:

"Do you really think that you really stand a chance against me especially without my brother awake? Do you even know how long he is going be stuck in the coma? You don't even know how to wake him up do you? You know the answers to only two of the questions I asked. The first and second question however are the questions that you need the answer to as soon as possible. I however can answer most of your questions that are going through your heads, but I won't. I will however answer you the riddle of the coma. To wake my brother is to bring him to a volcano and drop him inside, when he hits the lava he will wake up and then he will die, unless you place a spell on him that will teleport him right back to the top of the volcano. Now you are about to ask this question exactly like this, well now why do you suppose he's helping us instead of killing us when Twelve is in this blasted coma? Since I am in a generous mood I will answer that question as well. The answer is simple, because I want to fight my brother one last time when he is awake, but when he is in the coma I can't even touch his mind because he is blocked from the world. The last Lord you were with cast me out with Twelve's help and I haven't been able to break his barriers since. Now good bye and happy lava for it may be your last time to see Twelve alive which he is alive but you know what I mean." Nightmare asked and answered at the same time. Leaving everyone to ponder all he had said.

When we finally decided to take Twelve to the volcano SnakeWolfe pushed all of us from his body except for Agrognia who was studying Twelve's body as if she had seen it for the first time since she had been with us.

"What do you see Agrognia?" SnakeWolfe asked with confusion.

"SnakeWolfe Nightmare is lying to us, I know he is because a friend of my mother's went into this coma every time he heard his mother's name." Agrognia answered with a smile on her face.

"If you can wake him up then please wake him up Agrognia, pretty please." Joeker asked pleadingly.

"SnakeWolfe I need you to come here so I can tell you something in private and whispers?" Agrognia asked and said at the same time.

SnakeWolfe put up a spell wall that encircled the three of them, what happened inside I don't know but maybe you can tell us Agrognia? Joeker asked smiling.

"I suppose I could shed some light on this part of the story, um, but, well, ah what the heck, why not. Agrognia answered in a thinking way.

After SnakeWolfe put up the wall that encircled the three of us, I did three things, the first thing I did was get naked completely because the ritual that I was required to do required me to do that. The second thing I had to do was lay on top of Twelve and kiss him romantically. The third and final thing that I had to do was tell him how I felt about him in my heart, so I told him that I loved him and then he woke up and SnakeWolfe popped himself out of the circle and your dad and I had to have an adult moment with him.

"You mean you had sex? I thought you were only a child, how could you possibly have known what to do?" Areyana asked with disgust in her voice.

"The reason your father called me a child was because of how old he really is. Don't you remember, he's 5,300 year old. I was a full grown woman at the age of 6, which was how old I was at the time.

"So you see, by your mother's species' definition of adult hood, it is the age of 6, because they are full grown and fully matured, by that point in their lives." Twelve said while looking at his wife, and getting kind of excited.

"Oh I get it now." Areyana said with a look of understanding on her face.

"By the way yes we did and it was the most wonderful sensation we ever felt together, plus how do you think you were born?" Twelve and Agrognia answered her original question at the same time while laughing.

"Now that I can, I think I will finish the story since I have finally woken up once again?" Twelve kind of asked because Areyana had begun to look like she had questions that she wanted to let roll off her tongue.

"The questions I have Daddy are for you and you alone so I will ask them later." Areyana answered with a smile on her face.

After your mother and I had our moment together I knocked on the side of the wall and SnakeWolfe removed it, or some of it for Agrognia had not dressed yet. When she finished getting dressed she said OK we are good to go SnakeWolfe. He took down the last piece of the wall and then the three of us walked over to the rest of the party.

"Now that we are all together again, I take it that my brother Nightmare sent a hologram of himself to tell you all to bring me to the volcano to wake me up right? You were all smart to sit here and discuss the matter but I must tell you that I am glad that you let Agrognia handle the situation because I would have died, had you tried to wake me with the volcano lava. No matter how strong a spell the heat would have destroyed it, considering that volcanoes are one of Mother Nature's strongest children next to Mother Nature herself. I am glad to be back and Joeker you must remember that we are all friends one way or another in this group." Twelve said to everyone as a reminder that they were all in the group together to equal the party.

We stayed one more night at our current position hoping to get enough rest for the long trip back to the beginning where we had first come into the human world. It was a long night but not because of being attacked but because it was a sleepless night. Which didn't surprise me at all because we all had an adrenaline rush, that didn't go away which caused everyone only to get a couple of hours of sleep.

When they all woke up they packed up camp and then they hopped onto the dragons backs and then Twelve had to lead them to the right spot. You would think that traveling by dragon would take a shorter time but it actually took them longer because they got attacked by a flying pack of Cats. These cats are not like your normal house cat. These cats are as big as dragons, in fact every feature about them is like a dragon except for the fact that they have fur and they do not have the ability of fire breathing.

"Where did the Cats come from, I thought they were whipped off of the face of existence many thousands of years ago, how did they get here?" Agrognia asked herself out loud.

"They are here because Nightmare brought them here, or because he turned all regular cats into the Cats." SnakeWolfe answered with annoyance in his voice because he hated cats.

I jumped off of Oh-Halla's back over a hundred times and I still couldn't kill them all, it was like they were multiplying in mid air and then that's when I spotted Nightmare on the back of the leader Cat casting a healing spell called Invisaria Healaria.

"Everyone I have an idea of how to kill all of the Cats in one shot but I need you to distract Nightmare. Do whatever you can, just keep him busy long enough to do my idea. SnakeWolfe I need you to knock Nightmare off of his Cat and then when you get back watch what I do." Twelve shouted as loud as he could over the flapping wings and other noises from the Cats and the Dragons.

SnakeWolfe told the Dragon King what Twelve wanted them to do so the King started to fly directly at the Cats' Leader and half way to him he dived down and then when there was a foot or two feet left the King pulled out of the dive and then he started flying straight at the Cats belly. Nightmare didn't notice until after they hit. Nightmare went flying towards his castle. Meanwhile Twelve turned himself into a ball like Samus does in Metroid Prime, and then he had Oh-Halla open her mouth and swallow him whole. Now all she had to do was regurgitate him while blowing flames, turning Twelve into a Flaming Cannon Ball. It took Twelve and Oh-Halla five minutes to do this every time he came bouncing back to Oh-Halla. SnakeWolfe and the King did the same thing, it took them an hour and a half to kill fifty-thousand of the Cats when there was enough to equal three regular cats per person in the world, and there is a lot of people in the world.

It took us forever, well not forever but still it took us so long that we don't actually know how long. It could have been days, weeks, months years, we just don't know. The last thing I remember from that fight is that when I killed the last one of the Cats, I shouted at the top of my lungs these words: Is that all you've got brother, for you have lost but another fight by our hands. Are you going to fight one of us at a time or are you going to be a man and fight all of us at once, as in all together. Answer me Joseph-Omega, you coward.

When he finally answered my question, his voice caused all of us to jump up out of our skin and to get ready for battle, after two and a half minutes I realized that he was talking to all of us through his mind.

"Joseph-Omega is a name that no longer has any meaning to me now brother. Are you so arrogant brother that you would challenge me like that when you know that I could use the spell that trapped me into that cursed orb like ball. When I was in there I became so hungry for power that I started taking energy from the orb until one of the times that I started taking energy I caused a crack and saw daylight, after that I took as much energy as I could and then it exploded open setting me free. That's why your beloved home was destroyed in that retched cave of yours. Now I suppose you just figured out that the real reason your Geagle friend died. That is right dear brother it was not because she was the target, you were the target. She jumped in the way to save your life Twelve, that is also why the town was destroyed, or rather the reason it was destroyed was because you weren't there. Those blasted monsters, using the Edgewagan-Grankranieas, then again he was only activated when you killed all of the Grognogs it activated the brain system in Edgewagan-Grankranieas, which we both know that, that system is a computer that doesn't stop until it is destroyed completely. You my brother did a pretty good job of killing it but you only made it stronger because you cut it in half the way you did, the creature became two. I can see the look on your face and I want you to know, if you can't hear me already that I am laughing because it looks like you just figured out that I am telling you no lies today, by the way you have less than thirty seconds before those two Edgewagan-Grankranieas' find you." Nightmare said while still Laughing after he closed his mind to everyone.

Before they could hide the Edgewagan-Grankranieas' found them and then started attacking right away. The group didn't know what to do at first. They were confused and stunned from fear that had just woken up in their hearts that was never there before. When they finally gained the strength to move again Agrognia had already been stomped on and every bone in her body was crushed. If she hadn't been an immortal she would have died.

"SnakeWolfe give me your sword and I need you to make me a special weapon with your newest power that the last Lord taught you. This special weapon is called a Sword Crossbow. I will show you a picture with my mind of what it looks like. Agrognia I need you to create a shield around me to protect me from the two blasts that I am going to make with the Sword Crossbow. Oh-Halla and Dragon King I need the two of you to take the rest of the group the rest of the way to the beginning, where we first started the journey of the Lords and miles, I hope you remember where to go Oh-Halla because you are a dragon born from the imagination box that I have stored and locked all of my ideas, that are in my mind. Red head I am sorry that I can't remember your name right now but I need you to give me your two hair pins that you use to hold back your hair. Joeker I need you to give me a sense of direction on where the two creatures are coming from: North, they will be upon us when they reach the top of the hill over by that big building that looks like it would fall over from being touched and it also has a crap ton of broken glass as well: Thanks Joeker for pointing out the spot. SnakeWolfe have you finished with the Sword Crossbow yet?: Yes I have Twelve, here take the sword you requested as well.: Thank you SnakeWolfe, now Red head have you taken out your hair pins yet?: Yes Twelve here you go, I hope you have a good plan and reason for using my hair pins?: Yes I do but right now I can't and I also don't have enough time to explain it to you. Agrognia are you done with the shield that I asked you to create for me?: Yes Twelve I have finished the shield and I'm sorry to say that it will only protect you from one blast.: No it won't it will protect him from both of them because I added the second shield after you ran out of energy to use the same spell twice. SnakeWolfe said: Thank you, all of you for your help, because I would not have been able to do all of this on my own, it is an honor to have such friends like you. The whole group discussed and did the tasks in front of them"

Twelve loaded the Sword Crossbow and then the Edgewagan-Grankranieas' appeared over the hill that Joeker indicated.

"Alright you two freaks are going to die today and after I kill you I will burn your bodies until there is nothing left. Twelve shouted with vengeance in his voice.

Twelve was startled because he heard a voice that he never heard before, it was dark and deep and this voice also sent chills down his spine, which made him want to yell just from the sound of it.

"We do not wish to fight such a mighty foe that killed us in one slice, but we are under a type of magic control, some kind of a new spell that Nightmare created. This spell forces us to do what he wants no matter how hard we try to resist him and it, so we are sorry for bringing you pain. We ask you to do us a favor, and kill us completely so that nobody can use us for such evil ever again. The Edgewagan-Grankranieas' asked crying out for help, for their pain and their suffering to end.

"OK I will grant you such a favor." Twelve answered after he realized who was speaking he then threw up.

I started running forward very slowly at first because I was trying to load my Sword Crossbow, when I finally loaded it I took off the safety, and with this crossbow there are two triggers, the one towards the ass of the Sword Crossbow is the trigger to fire the sword, the second one that is in front is for zooming in, in case my target was really far away. After I loaded the crossbow I ran at full speed and as I was running forward I spotted one of the Edgewagan-Grankranieas and when I was a foot away I jumped and at the same time I did a forward flip. Time seemed to stop for a moment and then I saw the head and fired the sword. It was a direct hit. It fell to the ground and the head was gone. I turned around and started loading the crossbow again, but this time the Edgewagan-Grankranieas was not looking at me so I started at a sprint and then I ran at full speed, up its tail. At the last minute when I was about to shoot it shot one of the spikes on its back and I landed right on it. Then the Edgewagan-Grankranieas threw me off of its head and swallowed me. After I got swallowed I lost consciousness for a while.

"OK, so what happened after you got swallowed Daddy?" Areyana asked with a confused look on her face.

"I honestly don't know, I woke up hours later, but I was still inside the Edgewagan-Grankranieas' stomach, but I know someone who can answer your question. In fact he should be coming in any second." Twelve answered Areyana with a smile on his face.

"Uncle Joseph-Omega welcome back, how was your trip to Florida? Areyana asked with excitement in her voice.

Before Joseph could answer her question Joeker got out of the chair he was sitting in and then he opened the door and pushed Joseph outside. He started attacking Joseph without hesitation, and no matter how many times Joeker hit Joseph, he never hit him back. Joeker was about to kill Joseph when all of a sudden he heard a yell from inside the house.

When he looked up he saw Areyana in the doorway, and she said: If you touch my uncle one more time I will tear you into pieces, Joeker ignored her and then he punch Joseph so hard that his head spun around. Areyana took off her clothes jumped up into the air and changed, just like her mother and grandmother could and then she tore Joeker into pieces just like she said she would. When she was done she walked over to the porch changed back into her human form and put her clothes back on, like it was no big deal.

"When I say I'm going to do something I mean I'm going to do it and when I ask someone to stop I mean that I want them to stop, is that understood Joeker?" Areyana asked with a stern look in her eyes.

"Yes it is you little witch." Joeker answered with forced agreement in his voice.

Areyana just looked at Joeker, smiled and then helped Joseph into the house and sat him down in the chair that Joeker abandoned.

"My trip to Florida was great, extremely hot but great, thank you for asking." Joseph answered with a smile/grin on his face.

"We were wondering if you could shed some light on the story for us since you are here." Twelve said with a small smile on his face.

"Where did you leave off at brother?" Joseph asked happy that he could help.

"I left off with me being swallowed by the Edgewagan-Grankranieas." Twelve answered with disgust in his voice like he was trying to forget what happened.

"Ah ha I remember that, I remember that all too well." Joseph said between gaps of his laughter.

When Twelve became unconscious, I started pacing in my castle, thinking on how best to handle the rest of his friends. When I had stopped thinking I had actually made a hole that I fell through, of course I didn't notice because I was still thinking at the time when it happened, but when I was done thinking I jumped through the hole after I landed on the ground and then I sat in my throne. I had finally come up with a plan, and that plan was an extraordinary plan, so I called one of my servants, and I said: Wrog come here, there is something I need you to do for me.: Wrog said, Yes master Nightmare what is it you want me to do for you sire.: I want you to go to the volcano that is on the Hawaiian islands, it is on the north side of the island, and it is also the biggest volcano there you can't miss it.: What do you want me to do when I get there?: I want you to throw this letter into the volcano. A friend of mine that lives there wants revenge on a couple of the traitors from my brothers group. After you do that you will come back here by magic OK, is that understood. Yes my

Lord that is understood. When I gave him his orders he left right away. Color-row- Gragnog will be pleased to know that I have finally released him from his prison that Twelve put him in for so long.

I was so excited I accidentally destroyed my throne. I fixed it then I snapped my fingers and my guards brought my mother to me, and I asked: Hi mom how are you holding up?: You are a disgrace to our family you monster, attacking your brother and then trying to destroy the world, why destroy the world huh, you won't get more power or anything destroying the world. Your brother will stop you when he gets here, and when he gets here I hope that he traps or destroys you once and for all, because no son of mine should act like this, like a man who has lost the will to control himself. You became a man with power, and you became a man who has lust for power, a man who has power and wants more power will get more power but will only want and lust for more, a man who lives like that only gets destroyed by the power he has created for himself or someone else who wants more power will kill you and then they will be next so on and so forth. Oh and answer to your question, other than being held captive by my son, I'm peachy you flipping bastard.

I just sat on my throne watching her and once again thinking. I was thinking this time about what she said, for it is and was true, a man with power only wants more power and in the end he ends up dying because he had too much power.: So mother do you want to see where your favorite son is, hmm, because I can assure you that he is not going anywhere any time soon. Bring her over here to my All Seeing Glass Tablet. All Seeing Glass Tablet show us Twelve once again so my mother can see him for her own eyes.

This tablet is all glass and it is so thick that if you tried to break a piece of it off, it would break whatever you were holding. It looked at Nightmare then the woman the guards were holding, then Nightmare again and saw that he was shaking his head, then it blinked and Twelve was shown on the glass. He was still unconscious but he was having a bad dream. He was dreaming about what happened to him and then he woke up.

"There you go Twelve now you know what happened at my castle when it was standing." Joseph-Omega said with a pale face.

"It's OK Joseph you don't have to think about that any more. You're not like that anymore and I can see that you have changed a lot since you lost the lust for power after seeing what you saw, you killed the real Nightmare that was living inside your heart. You are now who you are because you destroyed the shell that you created, you have given yourself a better shell. Nightmare may still be my brother but he is in hell and he is not nightmare anymore because he became Skellingnasha which is his real name. He will never be able to hurt you again. Kids that, sound you heard was a volcano that went off, so don't say that name OK: they both shook their heads in agreement: good, now as I was saying, when you did what you did it caused Nightmare to change into something that could never be described without you wanting to die from explaining what he looked like. So smile and relax while I keep my story alright." Twelve said to comfort Joseph while patting him on the back.

"Your right Twelve, I am thinking and looking at it way too much, I think I will relax now." Joseph said with love in his heart.

After I woke up from my sleep, I realized where I was, and how I got there. The inside of an Edgewagan-Grankranieas is definitely something I would like to never experience ever again. It was the worst thing that could have ever happened to me. I started to try and think of a way out, but the only thing I had was the Sword Crossbow and the sword. I couldn't remember anything important to me at all and that started to frustrate me a lot. I rubbed my hands on my back in a spot that I thought

I had hit a rock when I landed inside the Edgewagan-Grankranieas, and my hand stumbled upon the hilt of a sword. I pulled out that sword and then I remembered everything that I was supposed to remember.

There must have been a spell on the sword because after I pulled it out I had an easier time thinking and I could think more clearly to. I held the sword in my hand and then I started thinking again, but this time I was going to come up with a plan. I couldn't use magic because of the magical acid in its stomach but I could probably cut my way out. I was about to do it when a man said: Stop, if your name is Twelveontia I need to teach you something before you get out of here. Oh by the way do you have any water I am thirsty as a hoarse in a desert?: Yes I have a canteen full of water, but how do I know I can trust that you won't kill me or something?: That's easy, because if I wanted to kill you I would have done so already: Good point, here you go, can I ask you something please, it's just that you look familiar to me so I wanted to ask you for your name.: You already kind of know who I am but I will tell you my name because you asked so decently. My name is Oh-Hogra, a long lost uncle, brother of your mother. Do you remember me now from Christmas ten years ago when I gave you that necklace that disappeared when you put it around your neck.: Oh yeah now I remember you, what happened to you ten years ago?: What happened to me ten years ago, huh, that's a good question, the only thing that I can remember ten years ago is waking up inside here.

They talked for the next couple hours. They talked about all of the things that Oh-Hogra missed, from the last ten years, and then they came up with a plan on how to get out of Edgewagan-Grankranieas' stomach. They tried to do everything they could but in the end they had to go toward its tail. They were thinking that it would have to poop eventually, so they just kept waiting as patiently as they could. It had been hours after they started waiting when all of a sudden they just fell down.

They were part of the poop, so the Edgewagan-Grankranieas just walked away. Twelve and Oh-Hogra waited till they could not see them anymore, then they climbed out of the poop, went to a nearby river and they cleaned themselves up. They couldn't get rid of the smell but at least they were clean. They walked to a field that had no buildings nearby, and set up camp for the night.

Chapter 18

UNEXPECTED

After my uncle and I woke up we packed up what little stuff we had and then when we were done packing up I told him how to get to the spot where my friends were, and we went our separate ways. I headed towards the hill that I saw the Edgewagan Grankranieas walking up, I was trying to see if I could catch up to it and then kill it this time but it was quite a few miles away and I would have to track it until I could find it.

Meanwhile, while Twelve was tracking down the Edgewagan-Grankranieas, his uncle was almost at the camp when Joeker came up behind him and put him in a head lock.

"Who are you and what do you want from us stranger?" Joeker asked, get a tighter grip when Oh-Hogra didn't answer the question right away.

"I am the uncle of Twelveontia and I want to stay at your camp until he gets back, and my name is Oh-Hogra. Oh-Hogra said while wincing from the pain.

"Can you prove that you are Twelve's uncle, because you could be a spy for Nightmare for all we know?" Joeker asked, ready to break Oh-Hogra's arm.

"Have you ever noticed the necklace that hangs around Twelve's neck, the necklace that he used to hold the Orbs that he collected from the brothers, well I gave him that necklace ten years ago." Oh-Hogra answered, with frustration in his voice.

"He's not lying to you Joeker, I can smell Twelve all over him, he must be telling the truth." SnakeWolfe said with a smile.

"I can tell you weather or not he's telling us the truth. If you really know Twelve, then answer this question. Who is he to me and me to him? If you really know him then you would be able to answer this question correctly." Agrognia stated with a smile.

"The answer to that question is that you and Twelve are lovers, in fact, with the power that I have, I can also tell that you are pregnant." Oh-Hogra answered happy that Joeker finally let him go.

Oh-Hogra walked around camp trying to find a place to sit, and when he did, Joeker sat right next to him, because he still didn't trust him.

"I sent him here because he is important to me and my family! Twelve shouted scaring everyone except his uncle, who fell off of the log he was sitting on, from laughing.

"You're here but how could you get here so quickly? It took me two days to get here and you arrived twenty minutes after me. The powers you got from the brothers must be flowing inside you like crazy?" Oh-Hogra asked with confusion in his voice and on his face.

"After I found the Edgewagan-Grankranieas I loaded the Sword Crossbow snuck around behind a pile of rocks, I waited there for five minutes and then I picked up a rock and threw it at a building. When the rock hit the building the Edgewagan-Grankranieas looked over toward the sound. I had just enough room to shoot it so I shot and at first it didn't look like I was going to get the head shot that I was looking for so I whistled and it looked towards me and then there was a big explosion. This explosion knocked me out for two in a half days, when I woke up I started running toward the camp, and yes the powers the brothers gave me is flowing through me, and it feels great." Twelve answered with the biggest smile on his face because he laughing a little bit.

Agrognia walked over to Twelve, took off her cloths, transformed and swiped his head off with her claws. It was only when he finally stopped laughing that she gave him his head back and as soon as he got his head back he kissed her.

"Where do we go from here, I mean do we just go straight to the castle and knock on the door saying hello?" Korgonagie asked with frustration in her voice trying to ignore their happiness.

"Why would you do that when you're not invited to my castle and not to mention that it is surrounded by all of my best worriers and monsters. So why would you be stooped enough to do something that stooped?" Nightmare asked asked while slamming into the ground with the Quake-impact, spell.

SnakeWolfe saw what he was trying to do so he through everyone into the air. He barely made off of the ground before the impact.

"How did you find us Nightmare?" Twelve asked ignoring what just happened and catching everybody putting them on the ground.

"It's not that hard when I can see all that happens with my All Seeing Glass Tablet." Nightmare answered with a smirk on his face.

"You broke the sacred law of laws, the law that is named Unexpected, how did you break it, it's a law that we read about in a book and in that book on the very first page it states that it is an unbreakable law, so I ask you again brother how did you break it?" Twelve asked in a pleading way, hoping that he would answer.

"How did I break the Unexpected law? I will tell you, I read the Book of Laws all the way through to the end and I found something very interesting, and that was a simple fact that at the end of the last chapter in the last sentence it said that it had been broken before and that if it had ever been broken again the person who breaks it the second time would lose their soul. So I broke it on purpose to see if that was true and i found out that it wasn't. Nightmare answered, while breaking into historical and uncontrollable

"You fool, when exactly did you break the spell?" Twelve asked noticing that something was very slowly starting to happen to Nightmare's body.

"I broke the spell a weak ago." Nightmare answered halfheartedly because he didn't care that Twelve still cared about him.

"So now we will see you at the castle when we get there, yes?" Twelve asked while thinking. (I wonder how much longer I have before his soul is taken and I can't save him?)

"Yes you will and I am going to give you the fight of your life brother so yo better be prepared. Nightmare answered while teleporting away.

"Does anyone know where I can find the Book of Laws, it's very important that I get my hands on it." Twelve asked desperately

"I have it in my backpack, but why do you need it?" Oh-Hogra answered with a questioning look on his face.

"I need it right now." Twelve said while grabbing the book out of his uncles bag.

"Okay." Oh-Hogra said still questioning Twelve's motive behind grabbing the book.

Joeker walked over to Twelve and used his emotions to bring out his swords Twelve looked at him and nodded his head in thanks.

"I can't believe it. My brother is such and idiot, and so am I." Twelve said smacking himself on the forehead like he did something wrong.

"What is, what's wrong?" Oh-Hogra asked recognizing the look that Twelve had on his face.

"Uncle I need to go to him, he's the only one who will know where to find the Book of Laws part two." Twelve said with the sound of aggravation in his voice.

"You can't, you promised your mother that you would never ever talk with him ever again as long as you should live, and last time I checked, you were still an immortal, and still alive. Be side's the only way to get to him is to go to Hell, and I won't let you go there." Oh-Hogra said while waving his arms around like crazy.

"I know, but I have no choice, he wrote the books and I need his help. I know I made a triple promise, the first promise was that I would never talk to him again, the second promise was that I promise not to break my promise, and the third promise if you might recall is that if and only if it's 100% necessary to break your promise you would consult with me first." Twelve stated. He still had aggravation in his voice but it was a little less now.

"Have you forgotten that your brother has your mother in his castle?" Oh-Hogra asked, shouting now because Twelve wouldn't drop the subject.

"I didn't forget, in fact, there is a way for me to talk with mom face to face. The reckless you gave her and I are still connected right, so maybe if I use a spell I can talk with her?" Twelve said with a smile on his voice, now that he found something that would give him the hope he needed.

"The only way your going to find the spell you created for doing that is if you can get your spell books and scrolls from Nightmare's castle, where he has them stashed away god knows where." Oh-Hogra said while still shouting and also spitting now.

"The thing that Nightmare doesn't know about is that I created a spell book that has a copy of each of my spell books and scrolls, I hid it in a very special place. All that is required of me is the password/voice recognition to work and I'll have it within a matter of minutes. I just hope that after 5000 years the ritual that I created to get it still works." Twelve said jumping really high into the air.

Twelve started passing back and fourth, thinking and thinking, while he did that everyone was confused and frustrated.

"Ah-Ha!" Twelve shouted unexpectedly, again scaring everyone.

The first thing Twelve did was whistle five consecutive times, then he shouted: I, Twelveontia request that the spell book I named Spellogshier, come to me into thy hands and make your presence known, with this password I beseech you, Future, Present, Past, Time, Twelveontia: With all of that, within two minutes Spellogshier came floating through a portal, and landed in his outstretched hands.

"How can a book, open a portal on it's own?" Everyone asked at the same time.

"Actually, I can answer that. May I answer their question, master." Spellogshier asked while floating in the air now that he was by Twelve's side.

"Yes you may, and don't call me master, your a friend I made to help me keep track of my spells so that I wouldn't lose them, and it's a good thing that I did because, my brother took them right out of our home." Twelve answered smiling at Spellogshier.

"Thank you. When Twelveontia created me, he gave me an auto spell casting system that makes it so I can travel through any and every portal. He also made it so that I could speak, and think on my own." Spellogshier answered with a smile back at Twelve.

"Spellogshier, do you remember the necklaces that I told you that my mother and I have, that have a magic connection, I would like it if you could find the spell I made that activated that connection?" Twelve asked with a serious tone in his voice.

"Give me a minute and I'll have that spell up on a page for you my friend." Spellogshier answered while opening himself and flipping through his pages.

It was the slowest minute in the world. It felt like an eternity, but when Spellogshier was finished he started ringing like a bell. Twelve walked up to him and grabbed him, and then the ringing stopped

"Invisible-Conestoga" Twelve cast onto both necklaces

"Doesn't he need to have his mother's reckless in front of him to cast it on both of them?" Korgonagie asked with a whisper.

"No they don't, because they already have an invisible connection, all he has to do is cast the spell and it will follow that invisible connection right to his mother's reckless" Oh-Hogra answered, also speaking in a whisper.

After about ten minutes of Twelve standing in one spot, he disappeared.

"I need some answer's and I need them quick." SnakeWolfe said putting his hands on the sides of his head like he was trying to hold it together.

"Okay, everyone get comfortable, because this is going to be a long story. Ten years ago, I was an entrepreneur, I traveled the world, and I've been everywhere. While on my travels I stopped at an old store called Pizza-Argo. This store carried everything you could imagine, and I mean everything, because if you imagined it, then you would be able to get it. When I got in there the first thing I did was imagine a cooked cheese pizza with an extra large Coca-Cola. The cashier sitting at the desk asked me for three dollars and fifty cents, so I paid him and then I sat down at a table and ate my pizza. When I was finished, I started thinking about what I had wanted to get my family for Christmas presents. When I was done thinking, I had bought everyone something special, but when it came to get Twelve and Jacky a present I was stumped. The cashier noticed that I was having a hard time, so he waved me over and told me that magical necklaces were pretty popular. So I started thinking about magic necklaces and found the two that I wanted. When I was done, I paid twenty dollars total for all of the Presents I bought. When I arrived at the party, everybody was happy and it was fun, everyone loved their presents. When it was over, I decided to finally give Jacky and Twelve their presents. I explained how they work and they both gave me a hug, that's when I disappeared." Oh-Hogra answered, grabbing a bottle of water and drinking the whole thing without stopping

"Well that answers a lot of questions, but that doesn't answer, my next question. How could Twelveontia and his mother Jacky have had those necklaces 5000 years ago? Korgonagie asked, still very confused.

"I think that I can answer that question for you actually." Spellogshier said while floating to Agrognia's lap.

"Okay, so please answer it?" Korgonagie asked getting impatient.

"Twelveontia and his entire family are exact reincarnations of Twelveontia and his family from 5000 years ago, so when they died, someone picked up the necklaces that were left behind and then 5000 years later, when Oh-Hogra was picking out Christmas presents, he stumbled across the necklaces You see, the reason that, that happened was because it was destiny. It was fate that he grabbed those necklaces, and five thousand years from now it could happen again." Spellogshier explained, happily.

Unknown to anyone, everything that was discussed at camp Twelve heard every word.

("Nice Job Spellogshier, I'm very proud of you and I'm also very proud of my uncle as well." Twelve said smiling.)

("Thank you, that makes me very happy. Should I let your uncle know or will you tell him when you get back?" Spellogshier asked cheerfully

("I will tell him when I get back, thanks again." Twelve said while still smiling)

("Okay, no worries then, I'll let you tell him when you get here." Spellogshier said in an agreeing manner.)

"What were you smiling about and why?" Jacky asked, because she had been interrupted

"Nothing. Sorry mom." Twelve answered with a start because he had forgotten what he cast the spell for.

"As I was saying before, I don't want you to go see your uncle Twitch, he went to hell because he messed with the laws of magic. He excepted his punishment and that's that. Now why is it so important that you go see him anyway?" Jacky asked in a pissed off way.

"Joseph-Omega, broke the law and now he's going to lose his soul, I know that Uncle Twitch took the second copy with him to hell, if I can get the second copy then I might be able to free him before time runs out." Twelve answered, hoping that his mother would understand.

"You may break your promise, but under one condition, you come back, understand." Jack said while giving Twelve a hug goodbye.

"Thanks mom, I love you and I will be seeing you again soon enough." Twelve said while he disappeared and then reappeared in the camp again.

Twelve explained everything, told his uncle that he was proud of him and then he teleport ed back to the town of the Dragon-Seers.

Chapter 19

Mortal

When Twelve got to the town, it was the same as before, beautiful Sarus was still there helping to guard the town, only now she was full grown. When she saw him she roared excitedly, happy to see him. He walked over to her and hugged her leg because that's all he could reach. Draggo saw Twelve and noticed that something was up but he didn't say anything.

"Draggo, how are you doing, it's been a long time, how have you been?" Twelve asked, while giving him a hug as well.

"Thing's are great, but I know that you're here on business, my wife saw a vision of you coming back when you left." Draggo said without the sound of surprise in his voice.

"You can't become mortal unless you die." Draggwina said before Twelve could even ask his question.

"The only way you can die is if you go jump into a volcano. If you want to die and go to Hell you are going to need to kill a friend or a family member, or someone you love. Good luck my friend you're going to need it." Draggo and Draggwina answered before Twelve could ask his next question.

He teleport-ed back to camp and explained what he had to do, everyone except his uncle tore his ear off, by yelling and screaming at him.

"Enough! My sister Jacky doesn't know that I'm still alive so I'll be the one he takes with him." Oh-Hogra yelled at the top of his lungs, which made everybody shut up.

"Oh-Hogra, are you serious, you can't be, I thought you wanted to see mom again?"

"I'm dying anyway, so it might as well be me, all right, I'm sorry I couldn't be there for you more." Oh-Hogra said chocking on his tears.

"Agreed." Twelve said also chocking on tears.

"I'll ask Cerberus to pick you up on the other side, so you have a guide." Joeker said holding back his tears.

Joeker closed his eyes and got a hold of Cerberus.

("Cerberus, I need you to do something for me, that I don't think is going to be easy for you?" Joeker asked.)

(What is it?" Cerberus asked, while walking towards him.)

("I need you to grab Twelve when he dies." Joeker said closing his eyes to help hold back his tears.)

("For you my friend I'll do it, but I need to know, why are you asking me to do this, they have minions for the job?" Cerberus asked, just now realizing that something was wrong.)

Joeker explained everything from the beginning all the way up to where they were at now.

("I see. I need the name of the volcano he jumps into so that I know where to pick him up." Cerberus said in an understanding way.)

"Twelve, Cerberus needs to know the name of the volcano, so he knows where to go to pick you up.

"It was named after the worlds greatest game that my world ever created, Halo." Twelve answered with a smile.

Joeker and Cerberus talked for a few minutes, and then Twelve and Oh-Hogra headed out to the volcano and when they got there, they climbed up to the top. Without the slightest hesitation Twelve threw his uncle into the volcano after cutting his head off. Twelve jumped in and killed himself.

"Welcome to hell my friend, I'm sorry that you had to go through all of this just to see your uncle Twitch, I talked with my king and he said that because your uncle Oh-Hogra sacrificed himself he sent him to heaven." Cerberus said while bowing his head to Twelve.

"This place is pretty gosh darn scary" Twelve said trying not to lose his nerve.

"It's a paradise for me, but I understand." Cerberus said respectfully.

Hell was full of the dead. There were endless walls of fire, and it was hot, very hot, like the inside of an oven hot or even hotter then that. There were three sections of Hell. What I described to you was the first section. The second section, was the same except for the river flow of souls, endless souls that lead to a waterfall where they were eaten by the all seeing and eating Serena, the queen of Hell. The third section, which was the main section had the castle.

The castle was painted red with the blood of the damned, and there were a hundred spikes that had hundreds of bodies hanging from each one, and when a spike is full the king comes out of his castle and eats them. Inside the castle there were those who were kept alive to be slaves, and serve the King and Queen for all of eternity.

"When I bring you to the King, there are a few things that you must not do:

- ☐ Don't make eye contact.
- ☐ Always keep your head down if you want to keep your soul and body.
- ☐ Remember that your rank means nothing down hear, only the King's does.
- ☐ Don't eat the food or you'll be stuck down hear forever.
- ☐ If the King challenges you to a fight, you have to except it no matter what.

Do you understand? As long as you follow these rules you should be okay, oh and remember to always address him as King or lord, like yes my King, or yes my Lord." Cerberus said with an extremely serious look on his faces.

By the time he got done explaining everything, we got to the gate of the castle. The gate was as tall as the world-trade center, and as wide as a mansion, and a hundred feet thick. They opened automatically, when they were done opening the king was sitting at his throne with his head in his hand and his elbow on the arm of the throne.

"your name is Twelve, I expected a lot more from a man of your ranking, please stand. I want to look upon the man who requested my council." The King said as if he was welcoming a long lost friend into his home to chat.

"But my lord, what about the rules, you will have to set them aside in order for Twelve to be direct with you." Cerberus said, shocked that the King would be so excited to see such a person.

"Triple J!" The King called.

"I'm here my King." Triple J answered, shaking out of fear from being in front of the King.

"Wright this down, today my five rules are dismissed." The King said with a real smile on his face.

"My King, I need to speak with my uncle Twitch, it's very important." Twelve said in a respectful way.

"I know that you need to see your uncle, and I'll lead you to him myself, but first we have to go to the arena, for the tournament." The King said, leading Twelve to a large open area that had ropes around it like a wrestling arena.

When they got there, there was a huge crowed of demons and devils and minions sitting on the benches that surrounded the entire arena.

"I want you to fight twelve of my strongest warriors, the first one is Red-Norma." The King said, while pointing for Twelve and her to step into the ring.

"But, my King, I must remind you that when I went into the volcano I lost all of my powers, how am I supposed to win?" Twelve asked with some concern in his voice.

"Don't worry, you wont have too much trouble." The King answered with a grin.

Without any further talking, the fight began. Twelve ran towards Red-Norma and did an upper cut. She did a back flip and then she kicked him in the gut. Twelve ran around her in a circle, feeling slow but nun the less ran around her anyway. She got confused and jumped into the air only to be knocked back into the arena. She didn't wake up, he had knocked her out with one hit.

"Your second opponent, is Red-Norman." The King said while clapping his hands.

Twelve was ready to fight this time. Twelve let Red-Norman attack first. Red-Norman did an uppercut with his sword. Twelve stepped aside and cut his head clean off.

"Your getting better, your third, fourth, and fifth opponents are, Crackle-Jackle, Shillong-Jay, and Sink Link" The King said still clapping his hands.

"Cerberus, is the King always this easily impressed, because I don't like that I'm being forced to fight like this?" Twelve asked while doing a ducking roll, jump, kicking Sink Link in the head, after doing a front flip to dodge his attack.

"Well actually he's usually yelling and screaming at people all day to do what they are told." Cerberus answered while pointing behind Twelve so he could dodge Shillong-Jay's head but.

"Well, then I guess I'll end these fights as quickly as I can." Twelve said while knocking Shillong-Jay, out with a kick to his stomach and a punch to his head.

"Your pretty good for 5000 year old human." Sink Link said, while jumping in the air and throwing ten swords at Twelve.

"Thanks, your very good as well, it's a shame your here in Hell." Twelve said while jumping in the air and grabbing hold of Sink Link, throwing him into Crackle-Jackle, which knocked them both out.(Whew, that was close, if Crackle-Jackle hadn't been distracted by that fem in, he would have dodged my next attack.)

"Nicely done, but you got lucky with your last attack Twelve, if Crackle-Jackle hadn't been distracted by the female demon, you would have had to fight a little longer. Your sixth opponent will be my daughter, Okinawa." The King said, while still clapping his hands.

"I'm sorry, but I can't fight a little girl, it goes against my code." Twelve shouted with anger, while taking a direct hit from Okinawa, which sent him flying into the demon crowd.

"Now I'm pissed." Twelve said while jumping into the ring, and then he jumped again, and slammed into Okinawa sending her straight through the ring.

"Holy Hell. I'm impressed that you could beet my daughter so quickly." The King said standing up and looking at the spot where Okinawa had been standing.(How can he be so damn strong, he was supposed to have lost his powers, and strength.)

"I'm sick and tired of these games my King so I will ask you to send the last six of your best and hope that I survive." Twelve said getting the hang of fighting in Hell.

"Twelve, are you serious?" Cerberus asked, surprised that he would make such a challenge.

"Alright, fine, here you go. Gorgoth, Forgon, Norefog, Frog-not, Bull-gotta, and Ax-hands, go to the ring and crush him." The King shouted angrily, because he was losing his patients. With his own game.

Twelve was out of patients as well so he gathered up what power he had and punched down into the arena, turning it into a giant hole in the ground, with no more warrior's. The King started to step forward but stopped when he saw his wife. The Queen was a giant just like the King. She was amazingly beautiful, she was big chested and the shirt she was wearing was see through, and she was wearing a skirt that was too short, showing her tiny panties.

"You have bested my husband's best men, and our daughter, you may pass through here whenever you like as long as you promise me one thing." The Queen said while shrinking herself to Twelve's size.

"I will make any promise you desire, as long as I get to see my uncle Twitch." Twelve said, bowing to her to show her respect.

("You must promise me that when we get alone time you will give me a son. If you promise to do that then you may pass in peace." The Queen said, while groping his ass.)

("I will only make that promise under some conditions." Twelve answered while groping her pussy.)

("Name the conditions and I'll see what I can do." The Queen said with a curious look on her face.)

("I will name those conditions:

- [ ] You teach me how to make myself big and small like that.
- [ ] You grant me three wishes of my choosing
- [ ] You promise not to tell anyone.
- [ ] I get to tie you down on the bed.
- [ ] You have to make it so I can leave when I'm done here, because the King isn't going to keep his word.

Twelve said, while trying to keep a straight face.)

The Queen didn't answer with words but with a handshake. She brought Twelve to his uncle Twitch and then let them be.

"I need the Book of Laws part two, or Joseph-Omega is going to lose his soul." Twelve said while grabbing his uncle and pinning him against the wall of his hell house.

"I guess you don't want to catch up on whats been going on?" Twitch said while twitching because he knew why Twelve was there to see him.

"Maybe some other time, but right now I need to get things done down here so that way I can save Joseph and save the world as well." Twelve said trying to keep his uncle in line so he wouldn't have to deal with his bull shit.

Twitch walked over to a trunk that he had and dug around to find the book, then he handed it to Twelve. Twelve opened the book and started reading it right away.

("Twelve, I'm terribly sorry to interrupt, but are you ready to experience an experience of a life time, because I am." The Queen said as she sent Twelve an image of her, getting ready for him.)

("Oh, yeah, I'm ready, just give me another five minutes." Twelve answered, as he sent the Queen an image of how ready he was.)

After another five minutes, he had read the book, and the entire book was copied to Spellogshier, as well. When he was finished the Queen opened a portal that lead to her bedroom. They were busy for forty-eight hours, which in hell is one day.

"These are my wishes:

☐   I wish to be sent back to earth, with my soul intact.
☐   I Wish never to be bothered by anyone from hell, except my son
☐   I wish to have my immortality back when you send me to earth.

Twelve said while getting dressed.

"I shall grant all of your wishes." The Queen said while still catching her breath.

Twelve was sent back to earth, and the first thing he did was cut his own head off to make sure he was still immortal. When his head popped back on he got up and teleport ed to the camp. When he arrived at the camp everyone was asleep, except SnakeWolfe.

"What do you think your doing!" SnakeWolfe shouted scaring the goosebumps out of Twelve.

"crap, I was hoping that you wouldn't notice me." Twelve said, while walking to the camp fire instead of the tent.

"Yeah well, it's impossible for anyone to miss you, man you stink like a cheap whore. What did you do, sleep with a demon?" SnakeWolfe asked while laughing because he was joking.

Twelve walked up to him and grabbed his arm and teleport ed to his old home.

"The truth is that, that was the only way for me to get out of Hell, so screw you man, and for the record it was the Queen." Twelve answered with an attitude because he was pissed about it.

"Holy shit, what in the fudge were you thinking, your going to get married when this is all over, not to mention that you have a child that will probably be born after you save your brother and the world." SnakeWolfe said while punching Twelve through the front door of the house.

"You don't think I know that. If I didn't do it the world would be destroyed, and I would be stuck in a place that I never wanted to go to, to begin with. I had to cast a spell on myself just to kill my uncle and jump into the volcano" Twelve said, with a thankful look on his face.

"What are you going to tell Agrognia when she asks you how it went?" SnakeWolfe asked while Twelve was hoping into the shower.

What Twelve and SnakeWolfe didn't realize, was that Agrognia heard every word. She was about to leave when Twelve started answering SnakeWolfe's question.

"You want to know what I'm going to tell her, I'm going to tell her the truth. If you don't be honest in a relationship right away, then you might as well not have a relationship at all." Twelve answered while praying that Agrognia's wrath wouldn't be to sever, and that she would forgive him someday.

"I'll forgive you, as long as you promise me that you wont ever do anything like that again, and if your son come's to visit you, I will gladly meet him." Agrognia said while jumping into the shower with Twelve.

"I'm going to go wait outside." SnakeWolfe said while rolling his eyes, and smiling.

After they were all finished at Twelve's old home, they got back to camp and they tried going to sleep. However, Nightmare was there, looking for Twelve.

"There you are brother. How was Hell, and uncle Twitch?" Nightmare asked with a grin on his face.

"Our uncle is doing great, and my trip to hell was a nightmare." Twelve answered with disgust in his voice.

"I know that you read the second book, so tell me, am I going to lose my soul or are you going to save me somehow?" Nightmare asked with cockiness in his voice.

"You will just have to wait and see." Twelve answered evasively

"So be it, I'll be expecting you and your friends, brother. Don't forget that.

"Don't worry, I won't forget, now why don't you go run along and setup your traps and what not, while I talk with my friends. Go on shew." Twelve said waving his hand in a shewing motion.

Chapter 20

NIGHTMARE'S CASTLE

After I left my brother and his friends I went back to the castle where I started to set up the traps, one for each of them. The first trap will be for that hot red headed girl. I think that I will have her fight an AK-Knall I will have Agrognia fight an Areregna Deer. That skinny one named Joeker will have to fight his sister Ana: I don't want to fight my brother: Why are you complaining, I am reuniting you with your brother you should be happy: I can't fight my brother because we have a blood pact, which means that we promised not to fight each other no matter what happens: That's OK because I will put a spell on you that will make you break that pact, now take her back to her cell, where she will have to wait until her brother's friends are knocked out.: Yes sir Nightmare sir: Thank you guards.: SnakeWolfe, what am I going to do about you I think that just because you will have the power of hell behind you I will have you fight the brothers of hell. Brothers of Hell come forth to me and obey your second master. Ah the red spot in the floor means that they heard me, good: You called for us master?: Yes I did, do you see that man with the two swords in the red and blue sheaths?: Yes we do master, what do you want us to do about him when he gets here master?: Well you see the problem with this one is that he has the power of Cerberus behind him, and I don't want him to reach me at all, so I will give you the power to take away his immortality: Sweet, Ahem we mean thank you master: Your welcome Hell Brothers, now go here and wait: Yes master: Now all who's left is you brother, I think that I will just fight you when you get to my throne room

An AK-Knall is a very strange animal that is a mix between a Minotaur and a three headed Cyclops. An Areregna Dear is a regular dear except for one significant difference; an Areregna Dear is pumped up with steroids and magical powers. Ana is just a regular human being. The Brothers of Hell are twins that died and went to hell, but their bodies are different from yours and mine. They are covered in flames and every time they say the word hell they cause fireballs to shoot out of the ground and walls.

At that time the whole group had reached the castle, and was trying to decide how they were going to get into the castle.

"I think that we should just walk in and see what happens after that." Joeker said with confidence that they would be okay.

"Oh yeah that's a good idea, why don't you just knock on the door and say we're here to kill you Nightmare for the love of heaven." Agrognia said with irritation in her voice.

They started to argue and then some of Nightmare's guards came out of no where and knocked them all out while they weren't paying attention. They were all dragged to the separate trapdoors that were set up, now that they were all asleep they would trigger the traps when they woke up.

"Now the question is who will wake up first, Wrog who do you think will wake up first?" Nightmare asked with anticipation in his voice.

"Well master I think that the red headed girl will wake up first but then again SnakeWolfe could wake up first because he never sleeps, so I think that one of those two would wake up first, master sir." Wrog answered with uncertainty in his voice.

"Hmm quite right, I forgot that SnakeWolfe is a lucky man with the extra organ that generates adrenaline and pumps it through his veins so he would wake up first, so the red headed girl would wake up second, then third would be the dumb ass Agrognia, fourth would be Joeker, and then the last person to wake up would be my brother." Nightmare agreed with Wrog, with an adopted voice of agreement.

Deep down at that time I was worried that Twelve would never wake up because he's a very deep and heavy sleeper, so while they were all asleep I called one of my guards over and told him to prepare the army for an attack. He looked at me dumb founded when I mentioned the word attack. So I told him like this, we are going to be attacked by their dragons. The guard jumped and then ran screaming get ready for battle you idiots, we are going to be attacked by dragons. Get the wall ready to withstand the flames of the dragons. You two get the army ready immediately.

While my guards got everything ready, I just sat in my throne and summoned my dragon and told him to take my form and take command of my army, when I need your help I will whistle, OK My dragon just shook his head and then left my throne room. Captain make sure that the men listen to my dragon, and if they don't tell them that they will be hanged or worse: Yes sir I will sir, oh um sir, I was just wondering why did you decide to capture your brother and his friends?: That my deer captain is the most wonderful question I have heard in a long time, the answer is easy, I want to see them fight for their lives, come and take a look in the glass tablet.: Yes Master Nightmare.

When the captain looked in the glass he saw how I set up the traps and then he left for the war that had finally begun. When Nightmare looked back at his tablet it showed that SnakeWolfe was waking up.

"Where am I and how did I get here? Where are my friends? Joeker, Agrognia, Korgonagie, Twelveontia!" SnakeWolfe shouted at the top of his lungs.

After about five minutes of looking around for an exit the only way to get out that he could think of, and see was a door in the wall that he had noticed when he woke up, from being knocked out for a few hours.

"It could be a trap but then again even if it is a trap it's the only way to go so oh well, I guess I might as well just walk forward." SnakeWolfe said, thinking out loud.

When he opened the door he fell through a whole that led straight to the bottom of the castle, and when he landed he was face to face with the twins.

"Hi we are the Hell Brothers and we are here to kill you for Master Nightmare." The twins said with flaming smiles on their faces.

Unexpectedly the twins ran forward and grabbed the left and right side of SnakeWolfe's body and then the three of them disappeared into Hell. As soon as SnakeWolfe realized that he had lost his powers do to the heat, he expected to be brought to hell though and whistled for Cerberus' assistance.

"The war has begun and now we will fight together." Cerberus said, while giving SnakeWolfe a little bottle that had his blood in it.

"Cerberus my friend, they have taken my power from me, so I hope that drinking my own blood will give me my powers back. So if this doesn't work I don't know how much help I can be to you." SnakeWolfe said while drinking his blood.

"SnakeWolfe they only took the power of immortality from you, so drinking your own blood should give it back. Other then that, they could not take your power of the sword because something drives you to your very limits, and the power within you is never going to go away because you have that power buried so deep that if you unleashed all of it at once you would destroy everything in your path, so use your power and kick ass." Cerberus said while grinning because he always wanted to test his metal against the twins.

"Your right, I will never give up no matter what, I have the power of anger on my side, there for I will win my battle with your help. SnakeWolfe said with confidence in his voice while thanking Cerberus with a nod of his head.

The brothers started laughing because they thought that SnakeWolfe was an ordinary mortal, and he would be easy to kill. They leaped forward, SnakeWolfe just stood in the spot that he was at because he was trying to become angry: I can't do it, I can't think of anything to make me angry: You here that brother, he's trying to become angry: Yes brother I heard him to, but it's not like his anger would help him stay alive against us is it: no it is not brother no, no: SnakeWolfe think about losing someone you love or maybe one of your friends: Your right Cerberus, I'm looking at the whole situation the wrong way and angle. Before one of the brothers could hit him he dodged the attack, his anger was building and building up inside of him and then he had a vision that Twelve had been killed by Nightmare, and after he saw that vision he willingly lost his control.

SnakeWolfe started laughing an insane laugh that would make a lunatic look like, and feel like an ant. With his anger out of his control SnakeWolfe becomes SnakeWolfe-Roarognorgan. When he becomes SnakeWolfe-Roarognorgan he sees nothing but his enemies, and right now he had the brothers of hell in his sight. He put his hands in the air and both of his swords flew straight up into the air and started on fire, one with blue flames and the other red flames.

"That's not possible to have that much power when you're a mortal, brother what do you think on the matter?" The Twins asked each other

"I agree with that, which you said but we can still beat him if we do the Hell Fusion. The Twins answered their own question.

The Brothers of Hell walked toward each other and when they got close enough they said: Hell Fusion, Lord of the underworld will you grant us the power we need to beat this SnakeWolfe-Roarognorgan once and for all.

There was a flash of flaming light that came from the underworld and somehow from the sun, when the light hit the brothers it caused them to become some kind of flaming beast on all fours. It had flaming red stripes and black stripes that shot spikes, and the creature's blood was some kind of poison, and acid mixed together. If anyone touches it then they will die, no matter if you are immortal or not, it wouldn't even matter if you were a god.

"What do you think of our new form SnakeWolfe?" The creature asked with both of the brother's voices overlapping each other.

"I think that you look even worse than your Lord Hell Fusion." SnakeWolfe answered while laughing.

After he said that the creature charged him and then their battle began. The first thing that SnakeWolfe did was transform into the SnakeWolfe he was born to be. When he transformed it scared the creature, but it lunged at him any way and with its claws it cut off a chunk of skin out of his right arm. He jumped into the air, and when he did, the time in the world just stopped completely, what he did was ask Cerberus what to do and he answered like this: We can't win this battle unless there has been a sacrifice to the god Hell Fusion. From what I can tell as well is that he wants you in the underworld with him, no matter what we do to this creature nothing we do to it will hurt it. But our agreement remains the same, I will make sure that it is honored by all of the gods, so what will you decide to do?

He didn't answer Cerberus because he wasn't sure what to do. As powerful as SnakeWolfe was he still couldn't do any damage to the creature just like Cerberus said, so he did the only thing that he could do. He hopped on Cerberus' back: Cerberus my friend I am sorry we couldn't work together, it has been the greatest pleasure I have ever had, but it is time for our Power Bomb technique to be active.: I believe you are right.

"Power Bomb explosion is required." They said at the same time.

When the explosion was done Nightmare was furious, because his best twins were gone.

"I can't believe that those two failed me, rah! At least SnakeWolfe is dead as well. Now who's going to wake up next? All Seeing Eye Tablet show me who will wake up next:

The Glass became a compass with the faces of Twelve's friends not including SnakeWolfe's face, it kept spinning and spinning, and it didn't stop spinning until five minutes passed and then it stopped on Korgonagie's face.

"Yes I finally get to see my son in action!!!!" Nightmare said with real joy in his voice.

When Nightmare first arrived in the human world he found a baby AK-Knall that had accidentally come through the portal and he raised it like a son, so now he wants to test his son's strength against the second best woman warrior in the universe Korgonagie, Agrognia being the first best woman warrior in the universe.

Nightmare trained AK-Knall to hate his enemies and to love and cherish him like he was a god himself. AK-Knall was taught all of the tricks that he could learn from Nightmare. So none of our friends know how powerful he can be because it's a mystery.

The room that she woke up in was called Drainear. This room is made of pure power, and if you were just a mortal you would die. If a regular human stepped into the room it would immediately suck the energy, and life out of you completely making you a sponge pretty much.

"I am AK-Knall son and humble servant of Nightmare, the ruler of the universe, once he destroys all of you and then becomes king of us all." AK-Knall said with a smile that would hit a home run.

"Nightmare will never become king of the universe as long as Twelveontia still has a breath in his body, and then when Twelve has won the battle against Nightmare the world will become normal again, and the world that we once lived in will be full of peace and happiness." Korgonagie said with a half smile on her face.

"Do you really believe in all of that bogus, I mean the only thing that is going to get you anywhere in this life, and in this world, is the power that we gain from crushing our enemies?" AK-Knall said still grinning but also losing his patients.

"All you are is a slave to your own power that you may have earned but you were also given that power through Nightmare as well, and too much power may kill you on the inside, because all power does is eat your heart and it also eats you alive." Korgonagie said with wisdom in her voice.

"No more talk it's time to battle." AK-Knall said with a smile.

Korgonagie tried to move but she couldn't move because she had been drained of all of her energy and now she is slowly becoming a sponge, which will end up happening to her for the next century.

"All gods of old grant me the power to escape this little force of power that holds me in this spot and also the powers to fight AK-Knall please." Korgonagie pleaded to the gods.

Before they could answer her prayers AK-Knall killed her in an unfair fight.

"Well at least my son didn't fail me." Nightmare said.

"What are we going to do? Joeker was in love with that human woman, when he finds out that we didn't get the chance to help her save herself. He would sacrifice all of his powers to have her alive again: Yes you are right there must be something we can do, what is it that you think we should do High God of old: I think that when the time comes he will come to seek us out at one of the secret sacred temples of the old gods and we shall answer him there and then, and only then, is that understood: Yes your Lord ship.

Chapter 21

A FAMILY BATTLE

"**S**o now who will wake up next my All Seeing glass Tablet?" Nightmare asked the Tablet in a greedy way.

The tablet started spinning like it did before but this time it moved slower, and then it started spinning really fast, and landed on Joeker's face.

"Brother you're finally awake I thought you would sleep forever." Ana said because she was in a good mood.

"What are you doing here, I thought that I would have to fight some giant one eyed ungodly creation? Which do exist I will have you know." Joeker stated, sensing that something was wrong.

"What are you doing talking to your brother? You are supposed to be fighting him, so get to it and if you win I will grant you the gift of immortality." Nightmare shouted with anger causing his entire body to shake.

"Then I agree." Ana agreed with understanding, and agreement in her voice.

Ana started running toward Joeker and she jumped on his shoulders, he was in too much shock to realize that he was being attacked and there for he just stood still. She pulled a small knife out of her back pocket and then she stabbed it into Joeker's heart. He didn't even notice, but he jumped back took out his sword and threw it at his sister, and when it landed, it landed into Ana's heart.

Joeker started to walk away because he thought that he had killed his sister but then he heard the sound of metal hitting the stone floor. Before he could turn around he had the blade of his sword sticking through the front of his body. When he turned around he reached out for his sister one last time, this time he grabbed her arms and thrust her into his chest with the remaining of his strength. After he did that they both collapsed dead onto the floor. His sister's spirit went to heaven and he was on his way there as well, but then the gods of old called his spirit forward so that they could speak with him.

"I take it that you have thought of offering me a seat with the council?" Joeker asked not surprised.

"No, we removed your immortality when you killed your sister. So we bring you here to explain something to you. Korgonagie your girlfriend was murdered because she had to fight in the room called Drainear. When she was brought there, she was unconscious so she lost her powers, if she had been awake she would have been protected by the shield that surrounds Mortal Gods such as yourself and Twelveontia, and the rest of your friends." High Lord God answered.

"So the only way to save her is to give up my powers and give them to her right?" Joeker asked, trying to be surprised.

"Yes and no, no because she is here in this realm of gods, and also, there is something you must do for us gods. Yes because the favor we ask of you will allow both of you to have your powers." High Lord God answered.

"And what is this favor you ask of us to do High Lord God?" Joeker asked with a smile on his face.

"The two of you must make love and then and only then will we send you both back with your powers. Before you ask why, the answer is simple, we are curious to see exactly how much love you have for one another." High Lord answered, with a smirk on his face, not expecting them to have enough love for one another considering that they hated each other when they first met.

We both agreed because we knew that the gods were honest, we made love to each other for five minutes in front of them but it felt like it was longer. When we finished the gods sent us back and we continued to help with the war, but before they sent us back they told us one last thing and that was that if either of us dies, they would not give us another chance to be with one another ever again They started walking into the throne room, and took a seat on the cold stone floor, which angered Nightmare.

"Warg, I need you to come here immediately!" Nightmare shouted.

There were hurried footsteps coming down the stairs.

"Yes master what can I do for you?" Warg asked.

"You told me everything you could about Twelve and his friends from the last 5,000 years and if you have then how come all of them except SnakeWolfe are still alive. So you have to explain to me how you screwed up or I'm going to kill you." Nightmare threatened with anger in his voice.

"I told you everything I knew at that specific time that I told you. When we went through the portal you told me that my work had been done and that I didn't have to spy on my old friend anymore, and you ordered me to stay in the castle master." Warg said with worry in his voice.

Nightmare spun around and cut Warg's head off.: That's what you get for repeating what I told you instead of telling me the answer that was on your mind you son of a bitch, now I'm pissed off.

Back then when I got pissed off about something I destroyed something in return, and when Warg did that I destroyed his home village and I tortured his family until they begged for mercy. To this day I regret my actions of anger and misguidance by my hate. My hate controlled me and I let it get in my way which started to tare, myself goodness apart on the inside, which caused me to let my hate kill me on the inside. That is how I became nice again; it was because my black heart was destroyed, then again there was a lot more to it than that.

"That's right, there is way more to it then that." Twelve and Agrognia said at the same time

The Areregna Deer was lying on its stomach with a sword in both hands waiting for Agrognia to wake up so she could kill her. As soon as she woke up she saw the Areregna and jumped up, but before she could do anything the Areregna started running toward her, then she jumped into the air, became a Tiger-Ragnar. A Tiger-Ragnar is when you become so intangible that you have the ability to control the other person's body. Agrognia collapsed and then the war began.

"So many memories, how do you understand your thoughts when they are swarming around and around like a bunch of bees trying to sting you Agrognia?" Areregna asked trying to stab a memory.

"This is the mind of a person who does not know how to control her thoughts but manages to do so any way. Who are you? I mean I know what you are but who are you? Agrognia asked and answered"

"I may be an Areregna Dear but my name is also Areregna, a servant of Nightmare, the all powerful and ruling master of the world." Areregna answered while still trying to stab one of Agrognia's memories

"Oh, well thanks for answering my question but it is, one of the most impossible things for Nightmare to become the master of the world unless he can beat his brother Twelveontia in man to man combat. Even you know that if Nightmare loses he will become the evil that clouds his whole heart, and when that happens he will become Joseph- Omega, Twelve's real brother." Agrognia said, trying to confuse Areregna.

After their conversation they started attacking each other with such violence that it would have destroyed the entire castle. Agrognia and Areregna were using all kinds of magic spells, when she finally won the war between Areregna's Thought Minions and her Brainorgas, which are a type of aura that protects the brain in case of being under some kind of attack. She stood up with a major headache, but none the less she like her other friends before her, who lived from their battles and such found their way out.

"Rah, I can't believe this, now my brother should be waking up any time now, let's see how it is going on the battle field." Nightmare said with an angry look on his face.

When I looked out the castle window I noticed that half of my army and minions together were gone and my brother's friends had joined the battle, and I was losing men quickly. Before the battle was over I poked my head out and shouted: anyone who retreats will be killed by my executioners before they step in the door, so you might as well turn your backs on me and then help my enemies. Everyone looked around towards the castle and then they helped my enemies get back into the castle.

"Now remember Twelveontia has to fight his brother alone then we can take care of the evil soul that he has created!" Agrognia and Joeker both shouted to everybody within ear shot and then those who were behind them and so on so forth.

Chapter 22

TWELVEONTIA AND NIGHTMARE'S BEGINNING BATTLE

I was dreaming for what felt like hours, I was dreaming about how I was going to save my brother and then I woke up.

"I must be inside my brother's castle, but I can't remember how I got here, the last thing I can remember is standing at the front of the castle trying to figure out how we were going to get in, we must have been hit in the head with a blunt object." Twelveontia said thinking out loud

"Yes you were hit in the head with a blunt object my brother and now you will die for your stupidity." Nightmare said as he threw a knife at Twelve.

After that Twelve sat down on the floor and crossed his legs, and started humming because Nightmare disappeared. He hummed until he was in a meeting with the brothers, and the Lords and Gods. Meanwhile Agrognia and Joeker waited for their signal, Joeker did the same thing that Twelve did.

"This meeting is now in session. Rod said.

"Hello Lords, Brothers and Gods of old my name is Nightmare. Nightmare said ready to cause death to anyone who gets in his way.

"Nightmare what are you doing in this place that is called the house of Good hearts, and how did you get here?" The high God asked.

"Oh High God you couldn't possibly believe that a man with an evil heart couldn't walk into a place like this, or do you?" Nightmare asked, surprised that they would be so naive

"Someone get him out of my presence before I lose my temper." The first Twelveontia shouted. Keeping his temper in check.

At that moment the second Twelve ran forward and then jumped into the air spinning like a torpedo toward his brother, knocking him off of the super sacred cloud, after making a whole in the wall of the place. Twelve was spinning so fast that it caused Nightmare to spin after being hit. When they broke through the clouds they were both on fire, and when they hit the ground they caused an earth quake that opened up a portal in the middle of the earth, but they ignored that and kept on fighting. Twelve did an uppercut while Nightmare did the same thing, when they hit they knocked each other backwards and lost their swords in the process.

They stopped themselves in mid air and flew straight at one another again and when they hit this time they caused it to rain. Their power shook the entire world, and yet again and again they went at it like typical brothers, in a normal fight. When they started using magic it started to snow, like somehow mother nature lost her balance. Spell after unspoken spell, without either of them giving up.: I won't give up my evil ways just so you can have a happy ending for yourself and your friends, just thinking of such a thing causes me to become sick to my stomach!: How come you won't except the truth?: What truth, there is no other life for me, the only thing that will happen to me is death and after that one hundred years of torture for the person that I have become?: The truth that there is a ritual that I can perform that will cause you to become a nice person again, and save your soul. All you have to do is give up your powers, and your immortality and then when the ritual is finished you will become immortal again, Nightmare you can't ignore your true heart!: I can do whatever I want Twelve because I have the power that can kill a god, so why should I expect anything else from anyone!?: Ah, you idiot, have you become so blinded by the darkness and evil in your heart that you can't see the love that your family has given you?: Love, ha what love, the only kind of love I got from mom and dad was leftover from when they loved you and your fucking perfection.: I guess I have to show you my side of our lives.

Twelve ran toward Nightmare, this time at full speed. When he did this Nightmare became frozen like an ice cube. Twelve then jumped into the air landed on Nightmare and then became frozen himself.

Now when my brother did this a whole ton load of family images from when we were very little to when I killed our brother who has no name. After the images stopped the both of them thawed out and were able to walk once again.

This time when Nightmare looked at Twelve he did nothing to harm his brother, instead he gave up his powers and his immortality.

"Brother I don't know how long I can hold back the evil in my heart, so whatever kind of ritual you have for me had better best be quick." Joseph-Omega said through the evil and darkness in his heart.

"Group are we ready?" Twelve asked, shouting his question to make sure that they were ready.

All of his friends said yes at the same time, now the ritual that they are performing is a very difficult one. They formed a triangle around Nightmare while Joseph-Omega kept showing himself to everyone. All of the soldiers and minions made a circle surrounding all of them. At this point Twelve and his friends had started to chant a Love song in a magical way. After they finished the song, four of Cerberus' slaves came and grabbed Joseph-Omega's evil side and ripped it from his body like it was a tape of some kind.

"Sweet I'm not evil anymore, I can finally see the light once again, and the darkness has finally become no more. finally that kind of power should be nobodies!" Joseph-Omega screamed with joy and excitement, happy that he was free.

"Hahahaahah, I'm finally free, no more being stuck inside that Prison of Unstoppable, no more having to listen to the damn worlds happy thoughts and moments, and no more unending happiness period, I am evil happy. To those who don't know who I am, my name is Gahulstrong-King!" Gahulstrong-King shouted with a joy that had evil intentions attached with it.

"Who is that man that just appeared over there on the top of that mountain?" Joseph-Omega pointed to the east as he asked the question.

"That is no man. Joseph that is the father of all gods, the god who created the gods, his name is

Xylotomy, and he is also the one who trapped Gahulstrong-King in the prison that he mentioned." Agrognia answered with awe on her face and in her eyes.

After his name was called he, teleport ed himself directly into the middle of the people that had started to gather into one crowed.

"Hello all of you, as my niece has told you, I am the father of all gods and that I had also trapped Gahulstrong-King in the prison that he described, but there is something that she did not know and that is that I can't trap him again, her and her friends have to do it." Xylotomy said with a look of shamefulness on his face."

"Father of all gods I ask of you, how may I be of service to you and your sons and daughters?" Twelve asked while getting down on one nee and bowing his head.

"Twelve please stand and the rest of you as well, may stand, you give me your respect just by welcoming me onto your humble earth. Twelve the only way this time to stop Gahulstrong-King is to kill him and that won't be easy. Use this spell on his back when you have the chance: Gogol-Oh-Hellal, do you understand?" Xylotomy stated, while bowing to Twelveontia."

"We all understand Xylotomy, and it will be done." All of Twelveontia's friends and also his brother answered at once.

"All of you within ear shot, I need you to listen to me as close as you can, and I need everyone here to make a straight line, I'm going to cast the spell Xylotomy told me to, but I am going to cast it on everybody's sword because it will do ten times more damage, so anyone who wants to live go home, and anyone who wants to die trying to re save the world stand in front of me." Twelve shouted while gathering up magic energy.

Everyone that heard him made a line in front of him and those who stayed and asked questions got into the same line. With all of the people and minions on the field there were one thousand of them total. Twelve started casting the spell on the swords one by one, and then his friends and brother also helped. By the time they were finished Gahulstrong-King had started attacking buildings and towns and everything else that had come back to normal after Nightmare was destroyed, and it had also become extremely dark outside. So our friends and extra friends slept till morning.

When we finally woke up half of the world had been destroyed again, which upset a lot of people.

"Here we go half of you go that way, because that way leads to the next city, the second half will go to the city that is on the left side of the road, my friends and I will stay in the middle, but anyone who finds Gahulstrong-King yell as loud as you can and one of our groups will get to you as quickly as we can." Twelve ordered.

"Gahulstrong-King is already here Twelve, look!" Agrognia shouted and pointed to him.

Twelve turned around and it would have been the last thing he would have done had he not been extremely fast. He dodged Gahulstrong-King's foot after it was an inch away from crushing him. Because everyone that didn't know how powerful Twelve was thought that he was dead, while the ones who had always known knew that he would still be alive.

"All right while I distract him everyone else just keep attacking his back, oh yeah and don't expect me to die that easy!" Twelve shouted as he made sure that Gahulstrong-King's eyes were on him the whole time.

One hundred hits later and everyone was losing their power that they had when they first started to attack, they were also getting scared because Gahulstrong-King would not go down.

"I shall grant all of you who are fighting Gahulstrong-King the speed that is necessary to beat him." Xylotomy said while getting ready to cast the necessary spell.

He cast a spell called Speedometer, and this spell granted anyone and everyone the ability of speed. After he cast the spell on everyone they were half as fast as Twelveontia. One thousand hits later Gahulstrong-King was finally destroyed and the world once again had been saved.

"Thank you all for doing a wonderful job helping me, now I shall keep the world from total kayos and darkness for as long as there is piece in people's hearts. If there is anything you have to ask of me don't hesitate to ask, because I will grant you one wish as long as it is within my power to grant it." Xylotomy said with a smile on his face.

Chapter 23

THE WISH

"Cerberus may we talk to you over here please?" Twelve and his friends asked.

"Of course you may." Cerberus answered a little confused.

They held a meeting inside Twelve's house, they talked for five or more minutes trying to figure out what to wish for. When they finally decided on what it was, it was nighttime, and the stars were once again shinning over head.

"Have you decided what your only wish is going to be?" Xylotomy asked with a smile that indicated that he had already sensed what that wish was.

"Yes we have, and we wish for SnakeWolfe to be brought back into this world because his journey has not yet been completed." They all said together.

"So shall the wish be granted as it has been wished for? Oh by the way he will return when the sun is highest on the beach within four days from now." Xylotomy said as he snapped his fingers and then disappeared never to be seen again.

"Someone is at the door daddy, I wonder who it is?" Areyana asked with some confusion in her voice.

"Knock, knock anyone home?" SnakeWolfe asked, while smiling.

"SnakeWolfe you finally made it to the house, and just in time too because it is your turn to tell a part of the story. I left off at when our wish got granted." Twelve said while patting SnakeWolfe on the back.

"Well I hope you made sure not to forget that you still have to tell about your mom and going to the beach." SnakeWolfe reminded him.

"Oh yeah that's right, thanks for reminding me about that part." Twelve thanked him with a smile.

When Xylotomy granted our wish and everyone had gone to their original homes Joeker tapped me on the shoulder and said that he could hear a voice coming from under a pile of stones, so I turned around and stopped to listen. I must have waited forever because I was still going through the fight with Nightmare in my head and then I finally heard the voice. I started to walk towered the pile that Joeker indicated and then it was louder. When I finally got to the pile I heard the voice so clearly that I shouted to the world: Mother let me get you out of here: Then I blasted away the stones and she walked out.

She walked right past me and my friends straight to Joseph and smacked him so hard that blood went flying along with a piece of his lip. The worst part about this was that she did it nine more times, just to make sure that Joseph didn't do anything like that to her again.

"I can still feel the pain from mom hitting me so hard so please don't talk about it, actually now that we have I'm itching again in the spot that I got smacked on." Joseph said with a big humongous frown on his face while scratching his lip.

Everyone started laughing and smiling making the day a lot brighter for each other.

It took us four days to get to the beach; we set up camp there just to make sure that we didn't miss SnakeWolfe's return. It was four days later when the sun finally hit the beach at the highest point in the sky. When we all looked into the water something started to rise and we all got our weapons ready.

When my head finally popped out of the water I shouted for Twelve and them to throw their weapons down, when they still had them up I grabbed my swords and when they lit up that's when they all put their weapons down.

"I finally made it back home with my friends and family, I hope that you guys don't mind if I call you family, do you?" SnakeWolfe asked.

"SnakeWolfe you know that I already considered you part of our family." Jacky said while giving him a hug.

"Let us go home and eat something for lunch and then later dinner." Joseph said rubbing his stomach because he was hungry.

"Jack we are home and we are ready for lunch, is the lasagna done yet?" Jacky asked, hoping that he didn't burn it.

"Not yet honey, but it has five minutes left, so it won't be to long of a wait. It's going to taste extra good this time because I didn't burn it." Jack answered.

"Dad that might be an even longer wait then you might think because there is something coming this way and I don't think that it is friendly." Twelve said concerned that the world was in danger once more.

The thing that was coming was something that was nothing to worry about.

"Sarus what are you doing here, I thought that you were guarding the town?" Twelve asked surprised.

"They sent me to come get you because they have something to tell you. It was so important that they wouldn't even tell me, so please come quick." Sarus pleaded while trying to catch her breath.

"Alright I will come but just to check it out, I can't stay in your world anymore without causing some kind of small problems." Twelve said while rolling his eyes.

I opened up the portal and thought of the town that Sarus stayed behind to protect and then we walked through it and I was attacked by an Ogre Double which is a type of creature that looks like an Ogre but has a skull for a head, and its body is on fire all the time. I just punched it and killed it in one hit.

"Twelve you're here, we got a message for you that we didn't know how to send to you in your world so we sent Sarus to get you and now here you are. Oh and here is your letter." Draggo said while lowering his head.

"I can leave now right, I mean I don't want to be rood but if I stay something bad is going to happen and I don't want innocent people being killed?" Twelve asked while getting ready to leave.

"Yes you may leave. All you need to do now is follow this letter to the letter exactly." Draggo said smiling, glad that Twelve excepted the letter.

So after I left I opened it and red the contents of it and it said:

Dear Twelve

I know that by the time you have gotten this letter you would have saved the world and also be home eating something that tastes good. The reason I have sent you this letter is because some years later from the day you get this letter to after the day you throw it away, you will be getting a phone call from a stranger that you have, and haven't met before, you must answer this call and then set up a meeting place in some kind of bar, after you set up this meeting take off the hood that he is wearing and then listen to what he has to say afterwards.

From: the Fortune teller. Are-Koon

PS: This will happen, quit a number of years later.

"Hmm I can't believe she remembered who I was after so many years." Twelve thought to himself, with a smile.

After sitting outside for five minutes reading the letter Twelve finally went inside to eat lasagna for lunch. They all had a good time and everyone slept very well.

Chapter 24

ONE YEAR LATER

"A year had past and everything was going just fine, nothing out of the ordinary." Twelve said to his kids.

"Mommy is the soup done, I'm hungry and from what I can tell my brother is too?" Areyana said as their stomachs growled for food.

"Yes it is, you all may come and get some soup." Agrognia answered, with a smile.

"So Daddy what happened after the one year past?" Areyana asked with a mouth full of food.

"Well after one year had passed by with nothing going on I ignored what my gut was telling me and went with my heart." Twelve said with love in his voice.

You see kids what happened during the year that went by was something very special because your father and mother got married together. You should have seen the looks on their faces when they realized what they had done, after they did it. It was one of the most beautiful days I have ever witnessed in my entire life. After their marriage they went somewhere on their honeymoon.

"Our honeymoon was the best one ever especially because I had a secret spot that I picked out personally, to make my wife happy." Twelve said while looking at Agrognia and smiling at her with extreme happiness.

"I can't believe that another year has gone by and still nothing has happened, no call or anything; Twelve I don't think that this is going to happen. Joeker said, with doubt in his voice.

"When Draggo gave me this letter and the person who wrote me this letter have never ever been wrong, so what if it hasn't happened yet, it's only been two years total since I got the letter." Twelve said without doubt."

"Well I know all of that but still you have to realize that there is always a chance that they could both be wrong and you know that." Joeker pointed out.

"That may be right for those who don't believe in fortune telling, I mean you have a good point but so do I." Twelve countered.

"I am sick and tired of you two arguing, you are both right, now can we get on with the day please?" Agrognia and Korgonagie said at the same time with frustration in their voices.

"Joeker if you don't stop this right now I am going to our home and I'm going to stay there for the rest of our marriage." Korgonagie said in a threatening way.

"Your right, Twelve I'm sorry for arguing with you, please don't hesitate to give us a call after you get this call from the stranger." Joeker said with an unknown look on his face.

After our wives broke up the argument that Twelve and I were having I left and that was the last time I saw him. He called every now and then but it was still a few years before he called me about the meeting.

"I'm sick of this waiting if I have to wait two more years later I am going to just start pulling my hair out every year I have to wait, starting next year." Twelve said with frustration while grabbing his head.

"Honey it will be OK I swear to you that you will get a phone call, next year, I saw it in a vision. Agrognia said trying to calm Twelve down."

"OK" Twelve said with doubt in his voice.

After breakfast Twelve and the kids went outside to play. What Twelve forgot about was that Agrognia's visions were seventy-five percent right. A couple hours later there was a phone call. Agrognia stopped chopping up vegetables and answered the phone.

"Hello: Agrognia thank god it was you who picked up the phone, it's me Korgonagie, your father just called us and said that your mother was sick and she needs your help, he said that she has been infected with some kind of virus that you had when you were a little girl.: You mean my step father and mother, and she is sick?: Yes I'm sure, she couldn't even hold the phone, your father had to hold it to her ear, so she could talk to me, she wants you to know that she is very happy for you and Twelve and the kids.: OK I will be there as soon as I can, by: Good bye.

Twelve walked in at the same time the phone was hung up, and when he saw the look on Agrognia's face he immediately started finishing up cooking lunch for her.

"Kids why don't you go up stairs and help your mother pack for her trip to grandma's house, she needs your help and I need it quiet down here in the kitchen, OK?" Twelve asked making sure that the kids did what they were told.

"Common kids you heard your father, now let's go up stairs." Agrognia said grabbing Areyana's arm.

Twelve and Agrognia mouthed the words I love you to each other, and then Twelve finished cooking up lunch and then the whole family ate at the table. When they were done eating Twelve and Agrognia put the kids to bed and then they asked their neighbors daughter to babysit them for a couple of hours. Then they left to go to the nearest city.

When they got there they hired a ship to get Agrognia to her step mother's house. When Twelve got her on board he told the captain to make sure that nothing happened to her. The captain said that he would keep an eye out in the open to watch and make sure she would be OK

"Agrognia I want you to right me a letter as soon as you get to your mother's house." Twelve told her after they kissed goodbye.

She just shook her head and waved goodbye, when the ship was out of view Twelve left for his home. When he got there he paid Verna for the couple of hours that his wife and him were gone.

"Don't worry sir there both still asleep, and I already checked on them five minutes before you got home." Verna said while waving goodbye.

"Did any one call asking for me?" Twelve asked before she was completely gone.

"Nope nobody called at all asking for you sir." Verna answered while closing the door and going home.

"OK thanks for staying." Twelve thanked her with all of his heart.

"(Knock, knock) Twelve are you awake?" Verna asked.

"Yes I'm home and the kids are still asleep so you shouldn't have too much trouble." Twelve said while heading out.

"OK, I hope you have a nice day at work." Verna said while getting a word search book out of her bag.

"Thank you, I hope I have a nice day at work as well." Twelve said while closing the door behind him.

Twelve closed the door and then walked to work, on his way he stopped at a book store to look for a book called Magic Masters for Areyana, when he bumped into a friend.

"Hey I know you, your Twelve, you're the guy who saved the world." Gorgon said trying to act like a jerk in a funny way.

"Holy cow, I haven't seen you since school." How have you been?" Twelve said and asked while shaking Gorgon's hand.

"Fine, fine, I have a family, heck you've probably come here to pick up a book called Magic Masters." Gorgon said with assumption in his voice, knowing he was right.

"Yes, yes I am but how did you know?" Twelve asked extremely curious.

"Because I have two girls that want the same book, and you are lucky because there just so happens to be three copies left, here take the third one." Gorgon answered, laughing a little bit.

"Thanks, so shall we buy them and get to work before our boss thinks that we aren't coming." Twelve said, also laughing.

They walked up to the counter and paid for their books. When they got out of the store they saw their boss standing outside with a copy of the same book, but he didn't say anything and the three of them went to work. Meanwhile, the kids and Verna were watching a TV show Cartoon Mania. It is a show where they play a whole bunch of cartoons to equal one cartoon, in one show.

"OK, kids time for your baths, who wants to go first today?" Verna asked, not expecting to hear anything.

"I will go first." Areyana said with excitement.

She took her bath and she loved it because she loved to be clean. Her brother however put up a fight, because he hated bathes with a passion, but in the end he ended up taking the bath anyway. Meanwhile Twelve was having a rough day at work.

"Rah, I can't believe how many times I've hit my thumb, it looks like the hand of a cartoon character of some kind." Twelve said blowing on it, trying to cool it down.

"Twelve, I need you to come to my office, its important." Twelve's boss called.

"Coming boss, just let me finish putting together this roof!" Twelve answered.

When he finished the roof for, and on the house they were building for a rich man in the city he went to his boss's office. When he got there his boss told him that he had worked plenty of hours that week and he was to go home until next week. So he went home and when he got home he checked the mail. There was nothing but bills, that he paid off.

"Kids, what kind of pizza do you want to have tonight?" Twelve asked while throwing his bills on the table.

"We decided that we want to have a super cheesy pizza!" Areyana said, speaking for her and her brother.

"Alright I called the Order Pizza to go and they said that they would be here in an hour." Twelve answered.

One hour later the pizza guy came and dropped off the pizza. After Twelve gave him the cash for the pizza the pizza boy left. After they ate the pizza they went to bed and had a great nights sleep.

The next morning when Twelve went shopping he bumped into a man while wearing a hooded sweat-shirt. When he got home he went on about his business like nothing happened.

Printed in the United States
By Bookmasters